A Cape Breton Love Story

A Cape Breton Love Story

RANDALL JAMES

Cover Concept:
Randall James

Cover Graphics:
Silke Stein

Cover Photograph:
Leslie Ann MacIsaac

Praise for
A Cape Breton Love Story

*"I'm absolutely loving the book. The characters make
me feel as if I'm right there with them! I'm laughing out
loud, love the surprises... and I don't want it to end!"*
Leslie Ann MacIsaac, Cape Breton, Nova Scotia

*"Every chapter captures my attention. Cannot wait
for the next page. The writing brings us right into the
story. Really enjoying it. Bravo!"*
Priscille Belliveau, New Brunswick

*"I love the story line and how all the local places and
traditions are incorporated. It truly is a Cape Breton
love story. I greatly enjoyed reading it."*
Pearl Egdell, *Cape Breton, Nova Scotia*

*"OMG, I loved it! The writing really got me into the
book. I can't wait to read what happens
with Logan and Rachel. 10/10. "*
Susan Odo, *Cape Breton, Nova Scotia*

Part One

Promise Me Forever

Prologue

Promise Me Forever

Logan Stewart
CHAPTER 23

Connor was crushed. The icy fog gripped him, as he stood at the Low Point Lighthouse, gazing out over the grey ocean — the little he could see of it. How could he have been so wrong? How could he have misjudged things so badly?

Jessica was gone and his heart was shattered into a million pieces.

He couldn't sleep last night, or the two nights before that. Early this morning, he'd come to their favourite spot where they'd expressed their deep affection for one another. That had been only one week ago. He shook his head. After that moment, he knew they'd get engaged, get married — would spend the rest of their lives together.

His mind flew back over the summer. He'd taken her to every romantic spot: weekends at Bras d'Or Lake and Louisburg, picking blueberries in the hills of Low Point, walks along the seashore and trips to the lighthouse. She'd responded as he'd hoped. He now knew she loved him, as he her. His goal had been to get her away from Brett so that she could see it, and he had. It was the summer of bliss.

But two weeks ago, Brett had reappeared in her life and begged her to go back with him. She'd confided to Connor about Brett's texts, calls, and him showing up unexpectedly wherever she was. Connor had tried everything to block Brett, had tried every trick, but Brett was relentless in his pursuit of her. Connor wanted to confront his nemesis directly, but Jessica wouldn't allow it. It wasn't her way.

Brett was beating him again. Brett had been better than him at college sports and academics, and even in the business world. But this was a far different battle. Connor just couldn't lose Jess to Brett. He just couldn't. And deep down, Connor was convinced that this was just another conquest for Brett. He would take great delight in looking into Connor's eyes, once he'd won her.

So, Connor needed Jess to see it. To see Brett for who and what he was. The problem, was that Jessica was nice. Far too nice and naive. She wanted to let Brett down softly, and Brett knew it, using it to his advantage. He was devious. He was also a two-timing creep. Connor had been the one to inform Jessica about that after he'd spotted him dancing at a bar with his secretary. How cliche. But that was Brett. If a pretty girl wore a tight mini skirt, he couldn't help himself. And yet, somehow, Jessica couldn't see it.

After Connor informed her, she finally confronted him. He had to admit it and then confessed to other affairs also. They weren't exactly affairs as they weren't actually married, but they were close to getting engaged one time, which is why Connor moved so fast. He knew that he was the best choice for Jessica and he planned on proving it. That was what this summer was all about. Connor could see her moving ever closer to himself with each passing day. Everything was working.

Then, a few days ago, she started to change. Her carefree spirit and laughter evaporated. She was in a constant state of thinking. What was bugging her so much? Deep down, Connor knew. Brett had gotten to her, and she was now deciding which man she wanted to spend the rest of her life with.

Connor had panicked a bit and pushed back on all the Brett stuff, which only caused a couple of arguments. There would be no forcing Jessica to make up her mind. Connor reminded her of the entire summer they'd spent together. She admitted she loved Connor, but what was unspoken in their arguments was that she cared for Brett also. That made Connor crazy. In his mind you could only love one person. *All* his fire, his flame, *everything* he had, was for Jessica. There was no one else and there never would be.

Recently, she was slow to answer his texts, and his calls went to her answering service. He felt the pit in his stomach. He had felt that before, when he'd been dumped years ago, in his early twenties. But he was now closing in on thirty. He couldn't lose Jessica. He just couldn't. But he had.

On Wednesday, she'd finally returned his last call, asking to meet at the lighthouse. He had shown up and she was already standing there. *Right here. In this exact spot.* He walked up to her and hugged her as they'd done a hundred times this summer. But he knew instantly that everything had changed. He stepped back and gazed into her eyes. At first she gazed back with a half smile, but then looked down.

He was devastated. He knew. She had somehow picked Brett.

"Connor, I have to talk to you."

"Save your words. You've chosen Brett."

Her eyes welled up.

"How could you? You know what he is. You know what he's done."

"He's says he's changed."

"Can a leopard change his spots?"

"We all make mistakes."

"Yes, but we grow and change. Not him. He's just tricking you."

"Connor ...."

"Look in your heart, Jess. Think of the summer we just had together. What more could I do to show you how much I love you. I know you love me."

She brushed a dark lock out of her eye. "I do love you, Connor, but I have feelings for Brett also."

He was exasperated. "You can have *feelings* for a dog or a bunny rabbit."

She laughed. He loved making her laugh. They gazed at each other. She looked away and then turned back, locking her eyes on his. "I've agreed to go on a one-week cruise with him. He begged me for one final chance."

"*Manipulation*! He will act like a saint on that trip and then propose. Don't say I didn't warn you."

"I'm so sorry, Connor. We're flying out Friday night."

"That was fast."

She looked down.

"Yeah, don't worry about it. I'll be fine." That was a lie.

She stepped towards him and they embraced. He grasped the back of her coat. Was this the last time he'd ever hug her? He started to shake, and cried on her shoulder.

"Please, Connor, *don't*."

"What do you want me to do? You're my soul-mate. The one true love of my life."

She looked up, her eyes wet. "I have to go, Connor."

He wiped his eyes. "Yeah, I guess so."

She slowly walked away, looking back over her shoulder twice.

He just stood there, longing after her. A solitary, pathetic figure. Dejected. Rejected. It was a living nightmare. When she rounded the lighthouse and was out of sight, he broke down, sobbing.

A fog horn blared, instantly bringing him back to now. He realized his eyes were moist. Well, what was he to do? He could throw himself into the sea, but that never helped anyone. He gazed out over the ocean one final time and turned to leave. And there she stood. At first he thought he was dreaming or having a mental breakdown. She was a dark silhouette, slightly hidden in the mist, but it *was* her.

"*Jessica*?"

She moved towards him.

"Jess?"

"It's me. I'm back, if you'll have me."

"*If I'll have you*? This is unbelievable. Inconceivable. What happened?"

"Can I have a hug first?"

He embraced her. Hugging her so tight, she gasped. Holding her arms, he stepped back. "Is it really you?"

She threw her head back and laughed. Gazing at him, her eyes filled with tears. Tears of joy. Tears of love. Tears for him. *For him*!

She moved into him, lifting her head, her lips parting. He bent down. Their lips met. And so did their souls. He was in Heaven.

After a minute, they stepped back from each other again, still holding onto one another.

"All your warnings were in my head every moment I was with him. I watched him like a hawk. And last night, when we boarded our flight for Miami, it happened."

"What?!"

"He had gotten us business class tickets. As we sat there and drank champagne, after having already downed a couple of drinks in the airport bar, he became chatty with the stewardess. He dropped his guard and struck up quite the conversation with her. It was like I wasn't even there. I even saw him checking out her legs while she waited on another passenger. He finally glanced at me, and realized I was staring at him. He made an awkward, funny face. Your words were echoing in my mind about him just manipulating me. I freaked out a bit, trying to quickly examine my options, and finally stood up and looked down the aisle. Passengers were still entering the aircraft in economy, so I told another stewardess that I felt sick and wanted to leave. Was it still possible? She said yes.

"Brett freaked out and shouted at me, demanding that I sit down. He was acting like a petulant child. They told him to calm down." She smiled. "Thankfully, it's still a free world. I grabbed my bag and exited. The airline even got my luggage off before the flight left. I took the next flight home."

"I'm so proud of you, Jess. You finally saw it. *Thank God.*"

She nodded, smiling. "I was so stupid for not listening before, when you were desperately trying to tell me. He had some kind of hold on me, but it's over. Broken. I see him for what he is."

He gazed at her. "I almost threw myself into the ocean five minutes ago."

"I would have followed you."

"I might have drowned."

"I would've drowned with you."

"You would?"

"Yes."

He gazed deep into her eyes and knew it was true. He grabbed her and they kissed again. Long and deep. They stayed in each other's arms for what seemed like forever. He had won her heart. And that was all that mattered.

1
Cruising

Rachel Abrams fastened the top button of her coat, as the cool October wind nipped at her. Standing on the promenade deck, the view of Cape Breton was stunning. She'd heard marvellous things about this island in eastern Nova Scotia, and so far, her friends were not wrong. Red and gold leaves reflected early-morning sunlight through lush greenery and rolling hills. Houses dotted the countryside. She returned to her cabin, as the *Jewel of the Seas* docked beside the giant fiddle in Sydney.

The cruise ship would be in town for one day and Rachel would have lots of freedom to explore, but she still didn't quite know what she was going to do. Maybe she shouldn't have come by herself after all. She had offers from friends and colleagues to accompany her, but in the end, had decided that what she really needed was some time all to herself.

Scanning her small wardrobe, she went with navy pants, a wine-red sweater and grabbed her fall coat. Stopping to look in the mirror, she examined her dark hair, which almost touched her shoulders. She really liked the shag she'd gotten before leaving New York. Her dark-blue eyes gazed back at her approvingly, as she studied her face. Maybe she was fooling herself, but she still couldn't see many wrinkles. *Not bad for forty.* She smiled. Once in a while, she could still turn a head. Satisfied with her look, she left the cabin.

A few minutes later, she walked off the ship. The first thing that caught her attention, besides the big fiddle and the Joan Harris Cruise Pavilion, were the rows of brightly coloured shops. She decided to start her adventure there as the little stores were already filling with fellow tourists. She browsed through a couple of them, which were selling t-shirts, mugs and many other gift items.

Rachel entered *Bree's Seaglass & More*, a small yellow shop sandwiched between a blue and red one. She noticed that they sold books and newspapers, besides sea glass jewellry and the usual trinkets. Stepping over to the sea glass displays, she admired some rings, pendants, and bracelets.

A brown-haired man in his mid-twenties, greeted her. She said 'hi' and kept browsing. Leaning against a bookshelf, she grabbed one book at a time and flipped through the pages. Most were written by an author named Logan Stewart. His genres were all over the place: science fiction, cozy mystery and even a romance novella. The blurbs were well-written and intriguing. And, even though the books were self-published, the covers were amazing.

She collected two paperbacks, a hardcover, and a tshirt with a lobster on it, and proceeded towards the same smiling man who stood behind the cash register.

"How are you today?" he asked.

"Fine. How are you?"

He started to scan the items. "Great. Just visiting?"

"Yes, I'm on the *Jewel of the Seas.*"

"Nice. Where're you from?"

"New York." She noticed his intelligent hazel eyes.

He nodded. "Welcome to Cape Breton."

"Thank you." She pointed to the books. "A Cape Breton author?"

"Yes, and the romance novel is a local bestseller."

"Interesting. Have you read them?"

"Oh, yes. I read most of what my dad writes. I might be biased, but he pens great action scenes."

She chuckled and tapped her credit card. "I'm looking forward to reading them."

The man packed everything in a bag. "Great. I'm always interested to know what tourists think of Da's writing. He needs a bigger audience."

She smiled. "Thank you. Have a nice day."

"You too."

Rachel spent the rest of the day on the boardwalk and checking out the many shops of nearby Charlotte Street. Afterwards, she returned to her cabin. She felt exhausted from all that walking, so curled up in bed with the novels she'd purchased that morning. She started to read the cozy mystery, *The Library Affair*, which was surprisingly good, but soon fell asleep. Awaking an hour later, she walked out to her balcony and gazed down at the giant fiddle and couples strolling along the boardwalk. She sighed. It had never bothered her that much before, but she now longed for someone to enjoy the evening with. Turning the big 4-0 was starting to weigh on her.

Shivering, Rachel went back inside and picked up the mystery novel from off her bed. She smiled. Tonight, she was dining with Logan Stewart.

2

One Year Later

The cool autumn wind blew through her hair, as Rachel, once again, stood on the promenade deck of the *Jewel of the Seas*. Rounding the cape, the ship closed in on the port of Sydney. Low Point Lighthouse came into view. The historic tower stood guard on a piece of land that jutted out into the ocean, crowned with a bright-red iron lantern. She smiled, recalling the last chapter of *Promise Me Forever*. The romance novella had moved her to tears. To think, that the final scene had happened right there. Connor had wanted to throw himself into that very sea. And there, Jessica had returned to him, appearing out of the fog. She sighed. *How romantic.* She made a mental note to visit the lighthouse if at all possible, and hurried back to her cabin.

A half hour later, and sporting a new red jacket, Rachel stuck her head into *Bree's Seaglass* and looked for the man who had waited on her last year. He wasn't present, but a young woman with baby-blue eyes and blonde hair was.

"Hi, can I help you?" she asked.

"Yes, I dropped in a year ago and bought a few books. There was a man behind the counter and we talked about the author."

"Oh, that's my husband, Mark. Let me get him." She headed towards the front of the shop and looked around the corner.

Two minutes later, the man, carrying a small box, entered. "Hi, can I help you?"

"Yes, I spoke with you last year about some books I purchased."

He set the box down and rubbed his chin.

She pulled out *Promise Me Forever* and held it up. "Your father is the author?"

"Oh, right!" He pointed at her. "New York?"

"Yes!"

"Back again, eh?"

"Yes, indeed, and mixing business with pleasure. Would it be possible to meet Mr. Stewart?"

"Business?"

"Yes, I'm an acquisitions editor for a large publishing house."

His eyebrows raised. "Wow. Da's a bit of a recluse these days, hiding in a local village called Low Point."

Rachel glanced at the author photo, realizing that the young man looked similar to his father. "Low Point?"

"Yeah — think green hills, blueberries, birch trees and a big lake."

"Sounds lovely."

"Yeah, it is, except when you get stuck there in the

middle of winter under three feet of snow.”

She chuckled. “Is it far?”

“About fifteen minutes away.”

“So, it’s not possible to meet?”

“Not these days. But ... well, to tell you the truth, I’ve been trying to get him out more.” He grinned. “What do you think about an adventure?”

Rachel put the book in her purse. “I’m in.”

“I’m Mark, by the way.”

“Oh, right!” She stuck out her hand. “Rachel Abrams.” They shook.

He raised his voice. “Bree!”

His wife appeared. “Yes?”

“This is Rachel Abrams from New York. I met her last year. She wants to meet Da and talk about his romance novel.”

“Nice.” She extended her hand. “I’m Bree.” They shook.

“Nice to meet you.”

Logan chopped down on another piece of wood, splitting it in two. Wiping sweat from his brow, he removed his blue-and-black checkered coat and threw it to the side. He grimaced — his back giving him pain — still not fully healed after all this time. He finished cutting the rest of the wood into kindling, gathered the pieces and brought them into the kitchen.

Walking back outside, he picked up his flannel coat and placed the axe inside the small red barn. He turned to his right and gazed at the hills. They’d sure gathered a lot of blueberries this summer. He smiled. Mark and Bree had come up on a few weekends and filled their buckets. Bree had then made blueberry muffins, scones, and pies — and had given Logan about half that she made. He loved that girl. Turning more to his right, he looked down White's Lane. The road disappeared into a sea of trees which reached almost to the shore, a half mile away. The dark-blue ocean was choppy on this windy October morning, the clouds moving fast across a blue sky.

Logan squinted as the sun peeked out between two clouds. He started to walk back to his small bungalow — white with blue trim — when he heard a car motoring up the road. He looked towards an opening in the trees and saw a red Toyota whiz past. He smiled. *Mark.* He waved as the car pulled up beside his blue Chevy truck. At first, he thought that Mark had brought Bree along, but now realized it was another woman.

"Hey, Da," greeted Mark, as the visitors exited the car and strolled up to him.

"Hey."

Mark gestured to the attractive woman. "This is Rachel Abrams from New York, in town with the *Jewel of the Seas.* This is my dad, Logan."

"Nice to meet you," they said in unison.

Mark scratched his forehead. "I met Rachel last year, when she dropped by the shop and picked up a few books."

"Oh," said Logan.

The woman smiled. "Yes, sadly, I only read *Promise Me Forever* a month ago ... but I absolutely loved it."

"Thank you." Logan glanced at Mark knowing there had to be more.

She continued: "I wanted to meet you and—"

Logan sized her up quickly: *Striking. Chic. City Slicker.* "Would you like to come inside? I've got a pot of tea on and a couple of muffins waiting for me."

Rachel smiled. "Sure. Sorry if I interrupted your breakfast."

"It's no problem at all," assured Mark.

Logan opened the screen door and his guests walked through the pantry and into the tiny kitchen.

"Where, Da?"

"Let's sit in the living room."

"You guys sit down. I'll bring the tea," said Mark.

Rachel chose the rustic grey couch, while Logan sat in his black leather recliner.

"So, what brings you to Cape Breton?" Logan asked.

"My friends have been here a couple of times and they always rave about it, so I had to finally see it for myself. The first time was last year. I fell in love with the autumn leaves, the ocean, the fresh air, and, especially, the people." She sighed.

"Yeah, I lived in Calgary for a few years. I really liked it, but Cape Breton has that small-town feel."

She nodded, gazing out the window at the view he'd seen a few minutes ago. Her striking eyes matched the ocean; her makeup just highlighting her beautiful facial features.

"Here we go," announced Mark, entering the living room with a tray of tea and cups. He followed that up a minute later with a bowl of muffins and sat in an old brown chair across from Logan.

"Help yourself," said Logan, pouring the tea.

"Oh, *blueberry*," said Rachel, after munching on one. "Another reason I love this place."

"My fave," said Mark.

Logan noticed his visitor still wearing her jacket. "Would you like me to start a fire?"

"No, I'm fine, thank you — quite comfy."

Silence filled the air for a few minutes as they ate and drank. Logan saw Rachel looking around the room and wondered what she thought of his small house. He'd left in the original wood panelling, and put in a new wooden floor, covering it with an oval grey-and-blue rug. He refurbished the fireplace and bought a new coal stove and microwave for the kitchen. Power outages were getting too common in recent years, so he liked being mostly off-grid when it came to heat and cooking. His two-bedroom home had all that he needed.

Rachel turned back towards him. "Logan, as I was saying before, I thoroughly enjoyed your romance novella: the characters, setting, dialogue, descriptions — everything. Well done. Is that the only romance book you have written?"

Logan glanced at Mark. "Yes, the first *and* last."

"Oh, I see."

"Yeah, my writing days are over."

"I'm sorry to hear that."

Mark sat his mug down and cleared his throat. "Da

wrote this one two years ago. Everyone loved it and wanted a series, but ...."

"But, that was the end," interjected Logan.

Rachel nodded. "I see."

"Yeah, and, well, I'm kind of retired now."

Mark shook his head. "Da, you're only forty-six!"

Logan chuckled. "Forty-five, but who's counting. I injured my back working in the oil industry out west, and, well ...."

Rachel frowned. "Sorry to hear that, Logan .... So, no hope for a series?"

"Nope."

Rachel took a last sip of her tea and set the cup down. "I actually work for a large publishing house in Manhattan and we're looking for fresh voices."

Logan turned towards Mark for a second who was staring at him, his eyebrows raised — as if to say, *"Are you getting this, Da*?!"

Logan returned his gaze to Rachel. "I really appreciate the kind words and encouragement, but—"

"I understand, and I'm not one to push authors when they're dead set against a project."

Logan smiled. He didn't really believe that was true. She looked like a woman who didn't give up easily.

Mark jumped up. "Well, Da, we have to get going. I told Bree that we'd only be an hour, max."

Logan struggled to his feet, his back giving him some pain, as Rachel helped Mark collect dishes and bring them to the kitchen.

Outside, Logan hugged Mark as they said good-bye.

"It was great to meet you, Logan," said Rachel, waving and ducking into the car.

"Same here," replied Logan, as Mark jumped in, turned the car around and headed down the hill.

"I guess I wasn't much of a help," said Rachel, looking out the front window as they drove the highway towards Sydney.

"Yeah, you can see how stubborn he is." Mark gestured left and right. "This is South Bar, by the way. We live just up the road."

"Nice — a lot like Low Point. Why did he stop writing, I wonder?"

Mark frowned. "Well, his writer's block seems to have started when Carly, his girlfriend, left him two years ago. They moved here from Calgary, but she was originally from Victoria. She was a bit younger than Da and somewhat snobby, Bree and I thought. Capers are a different breed. They like to kid around, *a lot*, and can be mouthy and blunt, but they're also kind, honest and will give you the shirt off their back. Carly didn't really give them a chance, so, she didn't really fit in."

Mark pointed to his right. "That's our place, right there."

Rachel viewed a yellow single-storey house close to the ocean. A long driveway divided a large green yard, leading from the highway to the house.

"Wow, right on the ocean."

"Yeah, that's good on nice days but terrible in stormy

weather. Bree doesn't like it when it gets too windy."

Rachel just nodded as she wanted Mark to continue with the main story.

"So, anyway, the whole thing with Carly really hurt Da, because we had all just moved down and he had this big fantasy of happily-ever-after built up in his mind. He loves this island and the people. Carly and Da started arguing all the time ... and then one day, he came home and found a note on the kitchen table. She was gone."

"Oh, that's terribly sad."

"Yeah. For all Carly's faults, he loved her a lot. Mark gestured again. "This is Whitney Pier. Famous back in the day for the steel plant. Towns like New Waterford, where Da grew up, and Glace Bay, mined the coal needed for steel making. The whole industry has been shut down since the early 2,000s."

"Interesting. I read some of that history in your dad's books."

A few minutes later, they arrived at the cruise ship parking lot.

Rachel turned towards Mark and smiled. "Thanks for the great adventure and for introducing me to your dad."

"No problem. How long are you here for?"

"Two days, I believe. The ship has an engine problem that they're trying to fix, so I think we're getting an extra day in port. They're updating us soon."

"Would you like to have supper with Bree and me tonight?"

"Sure. I'd love to. What time?"

"Come to our shop about five."

"Okay, see you then." Rachel hopped out, waved and headed towards the big ship.

Once in her cabin, she flopped down on the bed, musing on the days events and reached for the small romance book. Flipping through the pages, she stopped at the author photo. She smiled. "Well, Mr. Stewart, let's see if we can't nudge you along." She closed her eyes and thought about the ruggedly handsome man who lived alone atop White's Lane, Low Point.

3

A Game of Hearts

Sitting on the edge of her bed, Rachel stared at her shoe choices. She had no idea where they were going to take her. *Fall boots or high heels*? Both were black. She decided on boots to go with her black pants and magenta blouse. Grabbing her fall coat, she headed out the door.

Bree greeted her as she entered the shop. "So glad you're joining us tonight."

"I'm looking forward to it, but I forgot to ask if we're going to a restaurant or—"

"Nope! You're coming to our place."

"Wonderful."

Mark poked his head around some boxes in the back. "Hi, Rachel, be with you soon."

"No worries. I'm good.

A few minutes later, Rachel hopped into the back of their car, and not long after, they pulled off the main road and drove up the driveway to their house.

Walking to the front door, Rachel took a deep breath.

"The air here is so fresh."

Mark nodded. "Yeah, I don't think I could move back to a big city after living here."

They entered the house and Bree took Rachel's coat.

Mark walked into the living room and gestured to the couch below the large window. "Would you like a drink?"

"Sure," answered Rachel.

Mark smiled. "Wine, beer or coffee?"

"If you two are having wine, I'll have a glass."

Mark nodded and headed to the kitchen.

Rachel sat down on the cushy dark-grey couch and looked around. To her left, and at ninety degrees to the couch, was a matching loveseat. A matching recliner sat opposite her. Paintings of prairie landscapes, and photos, hung on beige walls, and to her right was a fireplace with a beautiful mantel above it. Past the fireplace was a large entrance into the kitchen. The house was quite a contrast to Logan's in size and brightness.

"Mark's a beer guy," said Bree, settling down at the other end of the sofa, "but I'll be joining you in a glass of vino."

"Great!"

A few minutes later, Mark served wine to the ladies, and took a seat across from them in the recliner.

Bree and Rachel clinked glasses. "Do you like fish?" asked Bree.

"Oh, yes, love it!"

"Good, we're having smelts, a traditional Cape Breton meal."

Rachel thought for a moment. "Hmm, I don't know if

I've ever had them."

"You're going to love them," said Mark.

Bree took a drink of wine and stood. "I'm going to throw them on now with potatoes and peas."

"Sounds sumptuous."

"By the way, I love your blouse," said Bree. "Very chic."

"Why, thank you."

"Must be lots of great stores in New York, eh?"

"Oh, yeah, Fifth Avenue has a zillion. Just ask my credit card."

Bree laughed. "Do you want to join me?"

"Sure."

The women strolled into the bright kitchen while Mark turned on the news.

Sitting on a stool at a small wooden counter, Rachel faced Bree's back as Bree whipped up supper at the stove. While they chatted away, Rachel swivelled on her chair and admired the kitchen. The top half of the walls were painted white; the bottom half were sea blue. A wooden table with four padded chairs sat below a window, and sliding glass doors led outside to a deck. The churning ocean seemed only a stone's throw away. She turned back towards Bree.

The kitchen filled with the wonderful aroma of the small fish. Sipping more wine, Rachel thought that maybe she *had* eaten smelts, a long time ago. "It's possible I've had these before. Can't remember when, though."

"Ah, the smell is getting to you."

"Yes — yummy, yummy."

"More wine?"

"No, better wait for supper. I'm already feeling good."
They chuckled.

While they chatted away, Mark sauntered into the kitchen and set the table.

Rachel raised her voice so Bree could hear her above the cooking noises. "I love your kitchen colours."

Bree glanced at Rachel over her shoulder. "Thanks. Mark and I painted the kitchen and picked out the appliances together." She sighed. "I hope we can keep the house after all the time and money we spent." She turned for a moment to face Rachel. "The down payment took most of our savings, and the mortgage and taxes are so high. We had no idea things had gotten so expensive in Cape Breton."

Rachel frowned. "In the States too. I'm sorry to hear that, Bree."

Bree took another swig of wine and filled both their glasses. "Yeah, the move from Alberta was expensive enough. We were just starting to recover from that *and* Covid, when inflation hit. I just hope Mark doesn't have to go back out west for work." She turned back to the stove.

Mark cleared his throat. "Honey, I don't think Rachel wants to hear about our problems."

"Oops," said Bree.

"It's totally fine," assured Rachel.

A few minutes later, Bree turned and raised her hands. "It's all ready!"

Mark gestured towards a chair for Rachel. As Bree served the meal, the doorbell rang.

"Who could that be?" Mark asked, as Rachel and Bree

took their seats across from each other. Mark threw the front door open. "Da! What are you doing here?"

His father smiled, stepped inside and closed the door. "Good to see you, too. Bree phoned and told me to drop by and pick up some smelts." Logan removed his boots and the men cut through the living room.

Sitting with her back to the wall, Rachel raised her eyebrows. The men walked into the kitchen, Logan wearing the same coat as earlier today.

Mark crossed his arms. "Bree, did you invite Da and forget to tell me?"

The night just got infinitely more interesting, thought Rachel, as she took another drink of wine.

Bree jumped up and hugged Logan. "Not exactly, Honey, but since he's here ...."

Logan and Rachel exchanged smiles.

Bree stepped back and looked at Logan. "Can you stay for supper?"

"I was just going to pick up the smelts, but if you've cooked enough ...."

Mark grabbed an extra plate. "We invited Rachel for supper."

Logan smiled again as Bree took his coat. "I can see that. We meet again Ms. Abrams."

"Indeed. Good to see you, Logan."

Once everyone was seated and served, Mark glanced at his father, who sat at the other end of the table. "Would you like to say thanks?"

He nodded and said a short prayer. Logan joined Mark

in a beer, as everyone enjoyed the delicious fish amidst lively chatter.

Mark leaned over to Rachel, whispering: "Bree sometimes forgets to tell me things, like inviting Da over. Sorry."

Rachel grinned. "I can see that. She's wonderful. I love her personality."

"Me too."

Bree took another sip of her wine. "Well, Da, Rachel told me all about her exciting work as an acquisitions editor for Big Apple Books ...."

Logan stopped chewing.

Here it comes, thought Rachel, as a mischievous smile tugged at her lips. Go, Bree. Bree appeared slightly intoxicated, which added to her easy-going nature.

Bree continued, quite innocently: "Are you going to write some new stories?"

Mark coughed as Logan put his utensils down.

Rachel took a second to glance at everyone at the table. It was like an unfolding play.

Logan managed a smile. "Nope, that chapter of my life is closed."

"Well, I for one love your books," replied Bree, who stood up. "Would anyone like seconds?"

"The smelts are succulent," replied Rachel. "I'll have more, please."

Rachel tapped Logan's arm. "I have to agree with Bree. You're stories are so moving and emotional."

Logan gazed at her, his green eyes playful. "Thank you.

And, I'm glad you don't push your authors when they turn you down."

Everyone chuckled in response to his answer.

"Another beer, Da?" asked Mark, hopping up from the table.

"Well, I should be going soon."

Rachel smiled. "Oh, please stay, Logan. The night is young and I promise to not mention your wonderful romance novel anymore."

"Yeah, c'mon Da, stay," agreed Bree, dishing out more smelts.

Logan rubbed his chin. "Well, that Canadian sure tasted good."

Bree and Rachel's eyes locked, as Bree picked up the wine bottle. "Would you like a top up?"

Rachel grinned and raised her glass.

After supper was finished and the table cleared, Mark asked if anyone was up for a game of cards.

"The only card game I know is Hearts," answered Rachel, "and it's been ages."

"We love Hearts," said Bree, who grabbed a deck of cards off the top of the fridge, and handed them to Mark.

"Da always wins," said Mark, shuffling the cards.

"That's not true," said Logan, *"only most of the time."*

"Well, we'll see about that," answered Rachel.

Logan chuckled.

"Is this the game where you give away your heart?" asked Rachel, not so innocently, and glancing at Logan.

"Hearts," corrected Logan.

"Yes, that's what I meant," she responded.

"And watch out for the wicked Queen of Spades," added Mark.

"Yeah, I've had enough of those," joked Logan.

Everyone laughed.

Rachel studied Logan. It was good to know that he could laugh about such things.

"Can I get a coffee, please?" Logan asked.

"You bet," said Bree, who put a pot on.

For the next hour, they played a couple of games, with Logan winning the first game and Rachel winning the next one. After some more small talk, Logan looked at his watch. "Well, I should be going. It was a great night. Glad I stopped by for a minute."

Everyone laughed.

"Do you want some smelts to take home?" asked Bree.

Logan stood. "No, I've had enough for now. Thanks for the supper, Bree."

"You're welcome, Da. Anytime."

Mark got up. "Um, Da, would you be able to drive Rachel home? I think I've had one too many."

"Um, sure, it's up to Rachel." They all turned to her.

She smiled. "I could get a taxi." *Why did I say that?*

"No," replied Bree. "You're our guest. We'll drive you home."

Rachel looked at Logan. "Okay, then."

They all walked to the front door.

"It's raining out," said Mark, looking out the window.

As Logan and Rachel put their coats on, Bree handed

Rachel an umbrella. "Here, you might need this."

"Why, thank you, ma'am." Bree and Rachel hugged and everyone said good night.

Heading out, Rachel popped open the umbrella. It was cold and pouring. Logan unlocked the truck and opened the passenger door for her. He held out his hand to help her in. She took it and stepped onto the railing and into the truck.

"Thank you, kind sir."

Logan closed the door and dashed around to the other side. "It's raining cats and dogs," he said, as he buckled himself in.

Rachel threw her head back and laughed. *"Raining cats and dogs.* I love that saying. Who came up with that?"

Logan chuckled, turning the truck around. They waved to Mark and Bree who were waving out the living room window. Soon, they were on the highway. The rain and wind beat upon the vehicle.

Rachel glanced at the driver. "Well, that was enjoyable."

"Yeah, they're a great couple. Mark found a gem."

"Can I ask a question about writing, as long as I don't mention *the book*?"

"Sure."

"What made you start writing?"

He thought for a minute. "Well, when I was in high school, I loved reading. One time, a teacher read my book report out loud to the class. That was the first time that I thought that I could write. But after I graduated, I joined the Air Force and got posted out west — to Cold Lake,

Alberta actually."

"*Cold Lake*?"

"Yeah. What a name, eh?"

She shook her head.

"True to its name, the winters were extremely frigid and we drank a lot. The next five years were a blur. I was just a young, stupid partier, who drank far too often. After that, I left the Canadian Forces and took a job as a labourer at a gas company. A couple of years after that, I got a job as an engineer's assistant at a large oil company. It was big money and crazy times, but six years ago, I fell off a ladder and injured my back."

"Ow."

"Yeah. And, well, long story short is, through all the medical treatments and rehab, I had lots of time on my hands, and I began to read again. I forgot how much I loved it. As I devoured books, I got a few story ideas of my own, which I wrote down in notebooks."

Rachel nodded. Maybe it was the wine, but the soft green glow of the dashboard instruments, the sound of the rain hitting the roof, the handsome man driving the truck, and the conversation on a subject she loved, gave the night an enchanting feel. *The dizzy, dancing way you feel.*

"And, that's when you wrote the romance novel?"

"I wrote that one about three years ago." The rain started to soften as they pulled up to the boardwalk. "Well, here we are."

She turned towards him. "Thanks for the drive home and for the lovely evening."

"Oh, you can thank Bree and Mark for that."

She smiled and gazed out the window. Although looking away, her thoughts were consumed by the man sitting next to her. He was so ... stable, friendly, and genuine. His thick, light-brown hair and dazzling eyes didn't hurt either.

"And what about you?" he asked.

She faced him. "What about me?"

"Well, how did you end up at a big publishing house? What attracted you to the literary world?"

She thought for a moment. "I always liked books. I read tons. I even wrote stories as a child growing up in Montana."

"*Montana*?"

"Yes, a small town outside Butte. Not too far south of Alberta. So, I know all about Big Sky Country. I grew up in the country. My dad had a few head of cattle and some milk cows, but later took a job at the post office. Mom was a part-time elementary school teacher. She raised my older sister and me." She smiled. "Some nights, we'd play a game. Mom or Dad would say a sentence and then each of us would add another sentence as we'd make up a wild story. It was such a great time. So, I've always loved storytelling."

He shook his head. "Wow, that's amazing."

"Yes, and even though I love my career and interaction with agents and authors, I spend far too much of my time dealing with the sales and marketing teams. I *hate* the bureaucracy side of the business. I *love* the creative side."

"I hear ya. I *love* writing, but I *hate* trying to find an agent or writing a detailed synopsis of each chapter of a new book. *Ugh.*"

"Yeah." She gazed at him. "Um ... you said *love.*"

"What?"

"You said *love writing.* Present tense."

He rubbed his chin. "Did I?"

She smiled. "Well, I should be going. It was nice to meet you, Logan Stewart."

"Likewise, Rachel Abrams."

He reached for his door handle, but she grabbed his arm.

"You stay right here. I'm sure I can reach ground safely." Rachel smiled, spun and opened her door. Climbing down, she waved and was gone.

Logan started the truck, but just sat there. He realized that he was attracted to her. It wasn't just her intelligent eyes and pretty face, but her hair, the way she moved — her gestures, her easy laugh. She waved again, and disappeared into the side of the ship. Logan shook his head. She was quite like a hurricane. He already missed her and hoped to see her again soon. But, wasn't she leaving in the morning?

4

Hide and Seek

After returning home, Logan called Mark. "What a great night. Thank you so much."

"Glad you had a good time, Da."

"I was wondering ... do you guys have Rachel's phone number and is she still in town tomorrow?"

"Let me check. Bree, do you have Rachel's number?"

"Nope. Sorry."

"She's still here tomorrow, right?"

"Yes, the ship has engine problems or something."

"Sorry, Da, we don't have her number, but she is here for an extra day. Did you have a good drive to the ship?"

"Yeah."

"Good, good. Going to ask her out?"

"Well, not on a date, but ...."

"You should, Da."

"Hmm. How will we get in contact with her tomorrow?"

"I'm sure she'll drop into the shop tomorrow morning. We'll call you."

"Okay, good night."

"Night, Da."

The next morning, a bright and calm one, Rachel appeared at *Bree's Seaglass & More* about ten thirty. Mark was busy with a customer, but Bree spotted her. "Good morning, Sunshine."

"Ha, ha. How are you today?"

"Bit of a headache, but otherwise, okay. You?"

"*Ugh.* Same."

"What are you up to today?"

"I'm not going out on any tourist trips. I'll just stay close to home, go for a walk and then visit some stores on Charlotte Street."

"Nice. I think Logan is trying to reach you."

That brightened her mood. "Really? Tell him to meet me on the boardwalk." She pulled out her sunglasses. "I'm going to need these, and a coffee. See you later."

"Bye!"

Logan's phone rang. It was Bree.

"Hi, Da. Rachel just dropped by. She's going for a walk on the boardwalk."

"Darn, I've got a load of coal coming, but the guy's late. Will be there as soon as I can."

"Okay — gotta run — tons of customers today."

Forty-five minutes later, Rachel popped back into the shop, which was still busy. She walked over to Bree, who was talking to a customer. As soon as there was an opening, Rachel said, "I'm heading to Charlotte Street."

As Bree rushed over to help at the till, she hollered back to Rachel: "I gave Logan your message."

Rachel waved. "Okay, bye."

A short time later, Logan pulled into the parking lot. He looked from the fiddle to the boardwalk, but couldn't see Rachel. He got out and walked on the boardwalk, heading left. He walked all the way down and back again, but saw no sign of her, so popped into *Bree's*.

Entering, he waved to Mark. "Have you seen Rachel? She wasn't on the boardwalk."

"Bree said she went to Charlotte Street. Sorry, Da, we're swamped. Hope you find her."

"Yeah, me too. Heading over there now."

Rachel enjoyed her late-morning stroll, window-shopping in a few stores. The one-way street reminded her of an old western town with two and three-story, wood and brick stores, only a few with awnings. It ran parallel to the boardwalk and was only a block away from the cruise ship terminal. Today, the street was bustling with tourists and locals. She stopped in a couple of gift stores, and later, browsed a ladies clothing shop. She tried on a couple of sweaters, but remembered that her suitcases were already jammed, so didn't purchase them in the end.

It was close to noon when she came across Daniel's Alehouse, a local pub. She stood outside and thought about going in, occasionally looking up the street to see if Logan might be coming. At that moment, a tall, dark-haired woman whom she had recently met on the ship, bumped into her.

"Hi, *Rachel*, right?"

"Yes, hi Jill."

"Isn't this a quaint little town?"

"Yes, love the Victorian houses."

"Me too, and the shops. I'm meeting my husband for lunch. Would you like to join us?"

Rachel tapped a finger on her chin. "Thanks for the invite, but I'm waiting for a friend." She looked up and down the street again.

"Well, I'm going to see if Ron already has a table. Hope to see you inside."

"Sounds good." Rachel waited another five minutes, then finally entered the pub.

Logan's back was aching as he walked down Charlotte Street, peeking into various stores to see if Rachel was shopping in any. He was starting to wonder if he should go back and get the truck. When he was just about to give up, he thought he saw her outside Daniel's, a couple of blocks down the road. As he squinted, the woman walked inside the pub.

He tried to hurry, but his back wouldn't allow it. A short time later, he entered the pub. His eyes adjusted to the light, as he strolled in. He looked around, spotting Rachel at a table, talking to a handsome, blond man who was drinking a beer. They were chatting and laughing.

Logan was stunned. He spun and walked out. *Well, that didn't take long.* Had he misread her last night? Maybe she'd just been overly friendly, or had too much to drink. Whatever the reason, it was a confirmation to him that he shouldn't give his heart away so quickly. What was he thinking? He'd been burned before. Twice. Fuming, he mumbled to himself all the way back to the parking lot.

Passing his truck, he stopped at the boardwalk, staring out at the water and sky. He shook his head and then headed for *Bree's*.

Bree spotted him. "Did you find her?"

"Yeah."

"What's wrong, you look like you just lost your puppy?"

"I should have known better."

"What?"

"I found her at Daniel's, having a drink with a man."

"Are you serious?"

"Yup."

"Da, listen to me. She popped in two times, hoping to see you. And don't you remember how she was last night? I think she likes you."

"Yeah, I thought so too, but maybe we just misread her friendliness. We don't actually know her."

"I'm sure there's a good explanation."

"Maybe, but I've been hurt too many times."

"Oh, Da."

"Yeah, plus my back is sore. I'm going home. Let Mark know."

"I will." A few customers entered and she had to break off the conversation. "I'll call you the moment I find out anything." She hugged him.

Logan limped back to his truck and drove home.

An hour later, Rachel dropped by the shop on her way to the ship. She felt exhausted.

Smiling, Bree walked up to her, while Mark manned the cash register. "Hi. Logan was here. He said he looked for you at the boardwalk and Charlotte Street."

"Really? How did I miss him. I looked everywhere for him."

"Yeah, and give me your phone number so I can reach you next time." They entered each other's numbers. Bree gently grabbed Rachel by the arm and escorted her around the corner. "He said he actually saw you at Daniels."

Rachel's eyebrows arched. "Huh? Why didn't he come in?"

"He did. He saw you sitting with a man."

Rachel thought for a moment and then laughed. "*He saw me with a man?*"

"That's what he said. He was not happy and went home."

"That *man* is the husband of a woman I just met on the cruise. His wife was in the washroom."

Bree covered her mouth with her hand and tried not to laugh. "Oh, my goodness."

"Yeah. What is it with *men*?"

"Good question."

Rachel shook her head. "All he had to do was come over

and say hi. We could have had lunch together. I can't believe it. I waited for him outside the pub for over five minutes, but couldn't see him, so finally accepted Jill's invitation to join them."

"Oh my goodness."

"Yeah. What am I going to do? I really like him, but this is ... well, crazy."

"Yup. A complete misunderstanding .... Do you have plans for supper?"

"No, just going to get some rest now, then pack up. We're going back to Boston tomorrow."

"Do you like pizza?"

"Oh, yeah."

"What kind?"

"Everything."

"Good. We'll get a couple. Meet back here at five?"

"Okay. Thanks for everything, Bree."

They hugged.

Bree looked her in the eye. "I'll fix this."

"Thanks. See you later."

Logan had just brought a bucket of coal into the pantry when his phone rang. He rinsed his hands quickly and grabbed it. "Hi, Bree."

"Hey, Da. Guess who just dropped in on her way back?"

"Rachel."

"Yup. I talked to her. Looks like you were right. She did indeed have lunch with a man."

"Ah."

"*And his wife*, who was in the bathroom. They are from the ship. She only met them a few days ago."

"Uh, oh."

"Yup."

He groaned. "I feel like such a fool."

"Yup."

"Does she know I know?"

"Maybe you should talk to her. I've got her number now, but I also invited her to pizza at five at our shop. Would you like to join us?"

"Yeah. That'd be great. I think I'll be having humble pie with mine."

She chuckled. "See you then."

"Thanks, Bree. You're the best."

Rachel strolled into *Bree's* a few minutes after five. Logan and Mark stood behind the counter and Bree sat on one of two chairs in the middle of the shop. They all greeted her.

"Have a seat," said, Bree, as joyful as ever.

Rachel sat down and gazed at Logan, who looked a bit sad.

He cleared his throat. "I'm sorry I missed you earlier today. I want to explain what happened, after we eat."

She nodded. "Sounds good."

"What time are you leaving in the morning?" asked Mark.

"I think it's around eight. Will double check."

"Dive in," said Bree, grabbing a slice of pizza.

Rachel stood up and took a big piece. The women sat back down.

After everyone ate a couple of slices, Bree gazed at Rachel. "Mark and I had a long day. We're going to say good night now and we'll pop by in the morning to say good-bye."

Rachel frowned. "I'm kind of sad to be leaving. I feel like I've known you all for so long."

"Yeah, you're part of the family now," responded Bree. "You better stay in touch."

Rachel lifted up her phone. "Oh, I will." As the ladies stood and embraced, Bree whispered in her ear, "He feels bad."

Rachel nodded as they separated.

Mark rounded the counter and gave her a hug also. "What Bree said is true. You're part of our family now. We want to see you again. I mean after tomorrow morning."

She smiled. "Oh, I plan on returning. You can count on it."

She gazed at Logan, whose eyes were locked on hers. She knew they had to clear the air.

Bree hugged Logan, and they left, leaving Logan and Rachel alone.

Rachel sat back down and gestured to the chair. "Join me."

Limping, Logan walked over and sat down.

She faced him. "What happened to your leg?"

He smiled. "Oh, I walked too far this morning, looking for an old friend."

She smiled. "Did you find her?"

"No ... well, actually I did."

"Oh, good. Where was she?"

"She was sitting in a pub."

"Was she alone?"

"No, she was chatting with a man."

"Oh, interesting. Was it her boyfriend?"

"I don't think it was."

"Tell me more."

His face flushed. "Well, I have to tell you, Rachel, I actually thought you were having lunch with him. I felt jealous and left. That's the simple truth. I feel like a ... well, I feel like a fool."

"Good. Because you were a fool."

He shook his head and looked down.

She reached over and held his hand. "Logan, it's okay. We all make assumptions that we later regret."

He glanced at her through his bangs, which were getting quite long. For a moment, she was sidetracked by how good-looking he was.

"Yeah, I regret it," he said. "We could have had such a good day together."

"Yes. I was looking for you and waiting for you everywhere."

"You were?"

"Yes. I really like you, Logan."

"And I really like you."

"Then *trust* me. I'm not the kind of girl who plays games. Not those kind of games. I'm not the Queen of Spades."

He chuckled. "That makes me feel great. I've been hurt so often. I don't think I can take it again."

She smiled. "Let's finish our pizza and go for a walk."

He brightened. "That would be great."

After locking up the shop, they strolled along the boardwalk and chatted. The sun was just setting. It was a perfect night for a romantic walk, although a bit chilly. They passed other couples, some of whom greeted them. After walking for a while, they sat down on a bench. The darkening sky was mostly clear with a few clouds, a quarter moon shone across the water towards them.

Logan faced her. "So, you're off tomorrow."

"Yes."

"I'm going to miss you."

She smiled. "I'll miss you, too."

"Are you sure I didn't totally blow it today?"

"No, but we should take it slow."

"Yeah."

"You probably have some trust issues after your past relationships."

"Yup. I told you. I'm not good at this."

She chuckled. "Who is?"

They stared out at the water and moon for a while longer. It was peaceful. She knew it was the perfect time and place for a kiss, but the jealousy thing had put a slight damper on things. She had a feeling that Logan was the right one — the prince she had waited her whole life for — so she wanted to do it right. And she knew that Logan also needed time to process everything.

She yawned and stretched. "I can't believe how tired I am. I guess I'm getting old."

"*Older*," he said. "Definitely not old."

She stood up. "Walk me back?"

"Of course."

She shivered, as a gust of wind blew through her. "Man, it's getting cold."

"Yup. It's that time of year."

As they walked, Rachel felt something drop onto her shoulders — Logan placing his checkered jacket on her.

She smiled, feeling like a princess inside. "Thank you."

He stood there in only a black long-sleeve shirt.

"Aren't you cold?" she asked.

"A little. But I'm not freezing."

She shoved her hands and arms into the sleeves, and wrapped her arms around herself, snug in his coat. "This is *so* warm. No wonder you wear it all the time."

"Yeah, I love flannel."

She laughed and thought of her dad. "Men always have their favourite coats or sweaters, don't they?"

"Oh, yeah."

A she walked, she smelled something in the coat. Rachel smiled and hugged the coat again. It was more than outside odours, or wood or a fire. She smelled *him* too. It was a nice, manly smell. Not like the pretty boys in her world, who always smelled of cologne and after-shave.

At that moment, they arrived at the big fiddle. They stopped and faced each other.

She gazed into his eyes. "Thanks for the lovely walk.

And, well, the whole visit."

"My pleasure."

"Oh, your coat." She started to unbutton it.

He put his hands up. "Please keep it."

"Are you sure?"

"Yes, of course."

"I'd love to have it. I'll wear it every time I'm cold. It will remind me of you."

"Yeah, the dumb lumberjack from Canada."

She threw her head back and laughed. "We don't all think Canadians are like that."

They chuckled.

"I'm going to really miss you, Rachel."

"And I you." She gazed at him. "Don't give up on your writing, Logan. Don't let anyone ever take that away from you. It is your gift ... from God."

He smiled. "Thank you. That's sweet of you to say."

She suddenly felt that she'd been too hard on him. "Could we have a hug before I go? Even friends hug."

"Yeah." He hugged her.

His big arms surrounded her. He seemed like a bear. She squeezed him tight and looked up. Her eyes moist. "I should go."

"Alright. Please return."

"I will. I promise."

"I'm gonna hold you to that."

"Do."

She squeezed him again, then walked away slowly, looking back a couple of times. She wanted to run back to him, but knew it wasn't the right time. She hoped she wasn't making a huge mistake.

Early the next morning, she stood on her balcony as the ship left port, waving to her new friends. It felt like she was leaving family. It was astounding how fast you could get to know someone. These Capers were such a friendly people. Not just Logan, Bree and Mark, but many she met were like this.

Bree blew her a kiss at the end, which she returned, laughing. She then locked her eyes on Logan's as best she could. Hers were moist. She wondered if his were. *Please bring me back soon.* They all continued to wave, until a few minutes later, when her friends were out of sight. She was now eager to see the Low Point Lighthouse on the way by.

As they cruised passed it, she thought about when she'd first arrived on this trip. She'd met the author just as she'd planned. And one day, she wanted to touch that lighthouse. She wanted to be there and gaze out at the sea and sky, just as Connor had done — just as Logan had done.

5

Back to Business

On Tuesday morning, Rachel entered her spacious office at Big Apple Books. Sitting on her desk was a beautiful bouquet of flowers in a turquoise vase. She hung up her coat, turned on the computer, and stepped to the window, overlooking the Hudson River. Cape Breton seemed like a distant dream. Had she really gone there?

A few minutes later, her assistant, Melanie, walked through her outer office and into Rachel's. "You're back!" she cried, stretching forth her arms for the hug.

Rachel realized how similar Mel was to Bree in height and appearance: both blondes and cheery — although Mel's hair was dyed and she often wore glasses. Circling around the desk, Rachel gave her a warm embrace. "Yes, I am, and ready to get back at it. And thank you for the lovely flowers."

Mel shook her head. "They're not from me."

Rachel's eyebrows arched. "Really, from whom then?" She sat down in her black leather chair.

At that moment, Nick Hoffman sauntered into her office. "Welcome back, Rache! I missed you. How was your vacation?" Nick always looked like he just walked off the cover of a GQ magazine. His thick dark hair, chiselled features, tall frame and tailored Italian suits had many women swooning as soon as they met him. Rachel had been one of those women, five years ago, when Nick first joined the company as a top executive. The fact that he was the owner's son, made him even more attractive. Rachel was long over him, though.

She smiled. "It was a welcome diversion, but I'm glad to be back. We have a meeting at ten?"

"Yep — Marketing and Sales have questions about *Christmas in Manhattan.*"

She rolled her eyes. "Oh, not that again. I thought everything was set."

"Well, we'll discuss it at ten." He turned to leave. "I hope you like your flowers." With that, he strolled out.

Rachel and Mel stared at each other, eyebrows raised. "*What the* ?" questioned Rachel, as Mel peeked down the hallway to make sure he was gone.

"Whoa!" said Mel, closing the door. "What was that?"

Rachel shook her head. "I have no idea. Has something changed since I was away?"

"Not that I'm aware of. Same old, same old." She lowered her voice. "I thought he spurned you years ago."

"Yeah, sort of." whispered Rachel. "It was mutual. And not only that, I met someone in Cape Breton."

"Really?"

"Yeah."

"Tell me *everything!*"

"I will, but not here. And I have the ten o'clock meeting that I have to focus on. Are you free to come over tomorrow night?"

Mel grinned. "Yeah!"

An hour later, Rachel strolled through sliding glass doors into the meeting room and sat in one of the white leather chairs. The cover of *Christmas in Manhattan* was displayed on a giant screen on the wall. Nick, who was also the editor-in-chief, sat at the far end of the long wooden table with fingers intertwined, watching department heads shuffle in and take their seats.

"Okay, let's get going," said Nick, glancing at his phone lying on the table.

Aiden from Sales held up a copy of *Christmas in Manhattan.* "I showed the new cover to my team and they still don't like it." Aiden looked like a librarian. He was middle-aged, mostly-bald and peered out at the world from behind oversized round glasses. He was put on planet Earth to oppose every book choice that Rachel ever brought forward.

Rachel tried hard not to roll her eyes. "What now?"

"It's too *Christmassey.*"

A chuckle escaped Rachel's throat. It was unprofessional. But thankfully, the design team and a few others others also chuckled and sighed.

"Too *Christmassey?* But it's a love story that takes place at *Christmas* in *Manhattan.*"

"That's another thing," said Aiden. "We need a more subtle title."

"We don't have any more time for changes if we want to keep next year's schedule," replied Rachel.

"Can't you give in on this one, Aiden?" asked Nick.

Rachel did a double take, as Nick didn't normally come to her aid. Her nemesis made a half-smile. He didn't dare oppose the owners.

After dealing with a few other issues, Nick leaned forward. "Is there anything else for today?" He seemed distracted and in a rush.

Rachel held up her copy of Logan's novella. "I might have found a new voice in Cape Breton."

"What genre?" asked Lena from Publicity.

"Romance — *not* steamy."

"Interesting. Are you going to get us a copy?"

"Yes, I'll get Mel on it."

"It's already on the market?" asked Mr. Negative.

"Yes, but like most indie books, almost no one knows about it. We could scoop it. I'm in touch with the author."

"I want to read it," said Lena. Rachel could always count on her. Lena had been with the company about five years longer than Rachel. She was tall and thin with straight grey hair and, at times, kind of like the furniture — just always there. But at moments like this, Rachel realized how incredibly supportive she was.

Rachel mouthed *Thank you* to her.

"Me, too," chimed in a few others. The support from most of the other leaders made up for life with Aiden.

Rachel was known for picking winners.

Nick knocked on the table. "Alright, get us ten copies right away. And Marketing, I want an update on all our big projects for this Holiday season, asap.

"Yes, sir," said Zach, as most stood up to leave.

Rachel and Nick stayed behind after everyone else had left.

"Thank you for the flowers, Nick." She tried to sound genuine.

He smiled. "You're welcome. Like I said, I missed you."

"That's sweet. But *flowers*? It will start rumours."

"Let them talk." His phone pinged. "Got to run. Mother wants an update."

Later in the afternoon, Nick dropped by her office, again. "Are you free on Friday night? I've got something important to discuss with you."

She felt uncomfortable. "Hmm."

"We'll go to *Frenchette*, your favourite restaurant."

Manipulation. "I don't know, Nick."

"I have a big decision to make for the company. I need your feedback. In fact, it concerns you."

"*Me*? How?"

"Friday night?"

"Alright." Thinking of Logan, she felt a bit guilty.

Standing at the living room window of her third-floor condo, Rachel looked out over her Stamford, Connecticut neighbourhood. The sun was just going down. She shook her head. Recently, another condo building had gone up close to her. The whole city was changing, and way too fast. It was already a growing financial centre, starting to rival Manhattan, and the population was growing leaps and bounds each year.

Still, she loved the city and Connecticut, especially her favourite spots, like West Beach and Cove Island Park. And she loved the scenery — the autumn leaves changing colour, and the distinct four seasons running into each other. She loved the whole feel of New England. In many ways it was similar to Cape Breton.

Maybe it was just turning forty this year, but on the way back from Cape Breton she'd done a lot of thinking. Thinking about Logan and his family. Thinking about Cape Breton. Thinking about Montana — her mom, dad and sister. And, now, Nick suddenly interested in her again after all these years? She couldn't put her finger on it, exactly, but she had the feeling that change was in the air.

The doorbell rang, jolting Rachel from her musings. She saw her reflection in the window and chuckled. She was still in her blue pyjamas and absolutely didn't care. It was that kind of day. She just wanted to be comfy.

"Come on in, Mel," she said, opening the door and hugging her friend.

"All dressed up for me?" Mel asked, sporting black leggings and a green sweater.

"Ha, ha. I think I still have cruise lag."

They entered the bright living room, where Mel flopped down on the dark-blue sectional.

"Are these new?" Mel asked, pointing to abstract prints that hung on the wall above the sectional.

The set of three reminded Rachel of large rocks — some turquoise and some black, on white backgrounds. "Nope. They were here last time you visited."

"Hmm. I love them."

"Me, too. The set has a cheery feeling." Rachel sat on the arm rest of a white chair. "Is this a wine or coffee night?"

"Coffee. It was a long commute. Work comes early."

"Smart girl." Rachel went to the kitchen, turned the pot on and returned, dimming the lights and settling in at the other end of the sofa.

Hugging a pillow, Mel grinned. "So, tell me everything. How was Cape Breton and *whom* did you meet?"

"Cape Breton was lovely. A picturesque island and salt-of-the-earth people. Their thick maritime accents are wonderful. Low population. Feels like living in the country."

"Nice. *And*?"

"*And* ... last year I picked up a few books from a local author, and this time I got to meet him. Logan Stewart. That was the order I gave you today."

She nodded. "What does he look like?"

Rachel grinned. "Aren't you interested in his writing?"

"We'll get there. What does he look like?"

"Handsome. One or two inches over six feet. Incredible green eyes. He's kind of quiet. Doesn't talk a lot."

"Wow."

"Yeah. And I met and spent time with his son, Mark,

and Mark's wife, Bree. She's a riot. Reminds me of you. Let me grab the coffee." She returned with their mugs full and sat back down.

"Does he only write romance?"

"He writes various genres, but what caught my attention was the romantic novella. It was so moving and set in Cape Breton. I think our readers would really like it. We'd have to spruce it up a bit and get him to expand the story or make it a series. But, therein lies the problem."

Mel took a sip of her coffee. "What?"

"He stopped writing a couple of years ago after a breakup."

"Oh."

"Yeah, but I think I can nudge him along."

Mel grinned. "If anyone can, it's you. That's your forte."

"Thanks. I just have to be sensitive. I think he's warming up to me a little."

"Oooo."

"Yeah, we had a fabulous meal of smelts at Mark and Bree's place and Logan happened to drop by." She laughed. "Bree and I drank too much wine, but it turned out good as Logan had to drive me back to the ship in the pouring rain. We had a wonderful chat. He's such a nice guy. Strong. Reliable. I felt like I had known him longer. Easy to talk to."

Mel raised her eyebrows. "Uh, oh."

"What?"

Mel leaned forward, hugging her pillow. "I think you're *falling in love*."

Rachel laughed. "Maybe."

"Mixing business and pleasure?"

Rachel took a sip of her coffee. "Yeah, hmm."

"And, what was that with Nick and the flowers?"

"Crazy. He dropped by later and invited me out for supper on Friday night."

"What?"

"Yeah, he said he has a big decision to make for the company and it involves me."

Mel put her cup down on the coffee table and gazed at Rachel. "Be careful, my friend. I just don't trust him. He seems to be moving fast."

"Yeah, I feel it too. There's something afoot that he's not revealing."

"I guess you'll find out Friday night."

"Yeah."

"Call me right after."

"I will."

On Friday evening, Nick sent a limo that drove Rachel to Frenchette. She strolled in and mentioned a reservation under Nicholas Hoffman. While she waited, she looked around. The soft lighting, and cozy booth area, created a relaxing and romantic atmosphere at her favourite restaurant.

Appearing a minute later, the manager brought her to a booth. "Would you like a drink while you wait?"

She sat on the inside cushy seating, leaving the chair on the outside for Nick. "Yes, a bottle of Chardonnay please."

A minute later, a young waiter poured her a glass and left the bottle.

A few minutes after that, her phone pinged.

Nick: Sorry! Will be there in ten.

She was famished and not impressed with Nick, so decided to order a steak and fries immediately. Frenchette's had the best in town. While she waited, she spent the time on her phone looking at photos of Logan, Bree and Mark. The meal arrived before Nick, so she went ahead.

The waiter stopped by again. "How is everything?"

"Excellent. Thank you."

He smiled and left.

Just then, Nick rushed to the table and sat down. "I'm so sorry. Had a meeting with Mother. He poured himself a glass of wine."

The waiter reappeared."Would you like to order, sir?

"Yes, I'll have what she's having. Sirloin steak — well done. "

The waiter nodded and left.

Rachel took a drink. "What's the big news?"

"You're looking at the new owner of Big Apple."

"What?"

"Yeah, Mom and Dad are stepping back and they want me to take full control." He raised his eyebrows and stared at her, expecting some incredible response.

She couldn't muster much, and still didn't understand how this would affect *her*. He was already, in many ways, the de facto owner at most meetings anyway.

She faked a big smile. "Congratulations, Nick."

"Thank you." He took a big swig of wine. "You're probably wondering how this affects you."

"Yes."

"Remember years ago, when we dated a few times?"

"Of course."

"Well, I wasn't ready to settle down. I was immature. But I've grown a lot, and ..."

"Yes?"

"Don't you see?"

"See what?"

"This is not just *my* future we're discussing, but it could be *our* future."

She put her utensils down and sat back. "Um, Nick." All she had thought about during her first week back in town was Logan. And, although they were roughly the same age, Nick and Logan couldn't be any more different. Logan was a man. A caring, tender, strong man. And Nick. Well, Nick was a boy in a man's body. And, although, sometimes that could be fun, Rachel was looking to the future and her plans, and Nick was not fitting, at all.

Nick leaned forward. "All I'm saying, is that I want us to start dating again." He tried to hold her hand, but she withdrew it.

Rachel leaned forward as her eyebrows knit together. "This is *not* a date, Nick." She pointed with her index finger to him and herself. "*This*, right here. *Not* a date."

He shook his head, as if stunned. "Well—

"No, we are two friends having dinner and discussing business. That's what I agreed to."

Nick took another big gulp of wine and looked for the waiter. He finally spotted him. "Hey, what's taking so long!"

"Sorry, sir, let me check."

Nick shook his head. "The service here is really going down."

Rachel shook her head. "You just ordered, Nick." She'd never seen him so agitated. She was starting to wonder if he was on something.

A short time later, the waiter reappeared with Nick's meal. "Here you go, sir. Sorry for the delay." The flustered waiter was obviously new. "Can I top up your wine, sir?"

"Bring another bottle," Nick said, as he cut into his steak. "Buffoons! It's *medium rare*." He threw down his utensils. "Take this away and get me the manager."

"Yes, sir." The scared waiter almost fumbled the plate taking it away.

A minute later, the manager appeared. "Yes, sir."

"The waiter is an idiot and the cook made me the wrong steak. I ordered *well done*."

"I am very sorry, sir. There must be a mix-up. We've had the same cook for five years. He is excellent. The waiter is in training. I will speak at him,"

"Perhaps he should find new employment."

"Nick!" Rachel whispered loudly.

The manager's face reddened. "Perhaps *monsieur* could be patient. We will correct the mistake and the meal is on us." He nodded and left.

Rachel assumed Nick's anger was a response to her

resistance. Did he really think she would agree to date him so quickly?

Nick gazed at her and smiled. A weak recovery attempt. "Sorry. Where were we? Oh, yes. You used to have a dream about owning your own publishing company, correct?"

That caught her off guard. "Yes."

"Do you still dream of it"

"Yes."

He cleared his throat. "Well, don't you see?"

"That's quite a leap, Nick. Is this a meeting or a marriage proposal?"

He grinned.

Her face flushed. "I wasn't expecting this, Nick. This is way too much, way too soon. I think I'm going home."

"*What? Why?* I haven't even gotten my steak yet."

"Well, I ate mine alone." She grabbed her purse, rose and put on her coat.

"At least let me drive you home."

"No, I'll grab a cab. Good night, Nick."

At the front door, Rachel tried to pay for her meal, but the manager wouldn't allow it. She pulled out a twenty from her purse. "Please give this to the waiter. I thought he was wonderful."

The manager smiled and took the bill. "Thank you, madame, I will tell him."

That night at Frenchette's seemed to have cooled Nick's heels, as he didn't ask her out again. For the next few weeks, Rachel put her head down and worked hard. And each day she thought about Logan, Bree and Mark. She toyed with the idea of surprising them for Thanksgiving — American Thanksgiving — but decided that would be too forward at this point.

Normally, Mel would pop over and they'd go shopping on the Saturday of the long weekend, but some of Mel's family had unexpectedly arrived in Rochelle, so she had to cancel. Rachel would just hang out in Stamford and visit her favourite places, alone. At least it would be peaceful and she could think about her future.

On Saturday evening, during Thanksgiving weekend, Rachel's phone rang. Joy flooded her heart, as she stared at the number. "Hi, Bree!"

"Hey, Beautiful, how's everything in the big city?"

Rachel laughed. "Busy, busy. I actually live in Stamford, Connecticut and commute every day to work."

"Nice. Wow. Got time for FaceTime?"

"Oh, that'd be great. Let me fire up the laptop. A few minutes later, there they were, face-to-face. "It's so great to see your smiling face, Bree."

"Likewise. Happy Thanksgiving, by the way."

"Thanks! You already had yours."

"Yup, eon's ago, in October. And all the turkey you can eat for a week afterwards."

"Ha, ha."

"Eek! Your coat!"

Rachel looked down and realized she was wearing Logan's jacket over her pyjamas. "Oh, yeah. I forgot. It's so comfy."

Bree grinned. "We're all here, by the way."

Rachel's face flushed and she felt butterflies. Bree moved aside and Mark and Logan appeared, waving.

"Hey, Rachel," said Mark.

"Hey, Mark."

"Hi, Rachel," said Logan.

"Hi, Logan."

Bree's head popped back in front of her. "We all want to know when you're coming back!"

"I actually thought about surprising you this weekend, but decided against it."

"You should have come!"

Rachel frowned. "Yeah, probably. I could kick myself for not calling you and planning it."

"How about you come for Christmas?"

"Really?"

"Yes!" chimed in Logan and Mark.

Logan pressed in beside Bree. "Come back soon. We miss you."

She had to resist the urge to kiss her screen. "And I miss you. All of you."

"Nice jacket," said Logan.

Hugging herself, Rachel nodded, gazing at his stubbly face, wishing so much she was there with him, with them. "Yeah, I love it. I wear it on cool evenings. Reminds me of a big lumberjack I know in Canada."

They all chuckled.

Bree sat in the middle again, with the men in the background over each shoulder. "Then it's settled — you're coming for sure!"

"Yes, just message me the date you want me to arrive."

"I will asap."

"By the way," Rachel said, "they owe me tons of vacation days, so I *could* come early."

"*Really*? How early?"

"Fifteenth? Twentieth?"

"Oh, goody. I'll message you later today."

"Great!"

"Okay, talk soon."

They all said good-bye and the Facetime ended. Rachel jumped up and studied the kitchen calendar, flipping to December.

6
Christmas

Strolling through the arrivals entrance of the Sydney airport, Rachel spotted Bree, who ran up to her and gave her a tight hug. "How was your flight?"

"Perfectly fine. I still can't believe they let me use the company jet. I'm so glad to be back!"

"Here, let me take a suitcase. The car is not far." They walked out and within a few minutes were on their way to South Bar. It was one week to Christmas and scattered flurries blew through the air. And, although it was only four in the afternoon, it was already getting dark.

Bree glanced at Rachel. "Mark's picking out a tree, as we speak. We wanted to wait until you were here to decorate it together."

"That's so sweet of you guys."

Bree cleared her throat. "By the way, are you Jewish? Mark mentioned to me last night that you might be. We thought we'd check to make sure you celebrate Christmas. Sorry, for not asking sooner."

"No worries. Yes, I celebrate Christmas and Hanukkah. I'd say I'm mostly secular, though. Hanukkah falls during Christmas this year."

"Really?"

"Yes. My father was Jewish, but Mom was a strong Presbyterian. The two holidays at the same time were never a problem for them. Growing up in Montana, we celebrated mainly Christmas, but Mom made sure there was always a menorah for Dad. That was the only thing he asked for, besides Christmas. I can still remember him lighting a candle each night and saying a little prayer. As far as Christmas, he was all in."

"That's so sweet."

"Yes, it was." She smiled. "Two things always happened in our house with Mom. No matter who you were, you got a full plate of food and you heard about Jesus. My parents brought home more than one straggler over the years."

Bree chuckled. "She reminds me of my grandfather. He lives in a small town outside Calgary. He's the same way."

"Sweet."

"Your parents are passed away?"

"Yeah, Dad passed away suddenly ten years ago, and Mom early last year. My older sister took care of her."

"I'm sorry."

"Thanks."

"Are you in contact with your sister?"

"No, not really. We became estranged over the years."

"Ah, that's too bad."

"Yeah. She didn't think I supported her that well when

my mom got sick and passed away. And then she had to handle the selling of the home and property. I was super busy at that time, and couldn't get out there as much as she wanted me to, so ... yeah."

Bree reached over and squeezed her hand. "Sorry."

"Thanks. She also has her hands full with three children and four grandchildren."

"Wow."

"Yeah."

Bree turned off the highway. "Here we are."

"Wow, look at that!" Standing in the yard, which was blanketed with six inches of snow, was a massive snowman, a penguin, and a few giant candy canes, all of them lit up. On the house, Christmas lights ran along the roof edge and circled the white posts just outside the front door.

Bree shut off the car. "We left the outside lights on just for you."

Rachel squeezed her hand. "Thank you, Bree."

Grabbing the suitcases, they entered the house. "Let's leave them in the entrance," said Bree, hanging up their coats. "We have your room all prepared whenever you want or need some private time. How about a cup of coffee?"

"I'd love a cup. Thanks."

They strolled into the kitchen, where Bree turned on the coffee pot. "I love your outfit. So chic."

"Thanks!" Rachel wore a navy-blue business jacket with matching pants, and a white turtleneck. "And I love your blouse."

"Yes, magenta. Inspired by a friend of mine."

Rachel laughed. "I think I wore something similar last time I was here."

"Yes, you did. Now, tell me all about New York. What have you been doing the past couple of months?"

Unbuttoning her jacket, Rachel sat down at the table. "Mostly arguing with Sales and Marketing and pushing my favourite authors and books, including Logan's. I'm so looking forward to this downtime."

"By the way, something I wanted to ask you before ... have you ever had any serious relationships in New York?"

"Ha, ha. You remind me of Melanie, my friend in New York. When it comes to romance, she wants *all* the details. As long as it's about me."

Bree grinned. "Well?"

"There's not much to tell. I did have some dates over the years, but none of them really developed into anything serious."

Bree set mugs, cream and sugar on the table. "Come on. You're a pretty, dynamic, acquisitions editor of a major firm. Surely you've had some suitors over the years."

"Um, not really. As you can tell, I'm married to my career."

Bree poured the coffee and sat down. "Hmm."

Rachel gazed at her. "Well, there was one man who showed some serious interest, but it's a long story and I'm trying to figure him out."

"*Oh, goody.* Tell me about him."

"Okay, but don't say anything to Logan, just yet. His name is Nick, the owner's son. He's tall, handsome, dark hair and eyes, and, when he first joined Big Apple, about five years ago, I had a *huge* crush on him. A few years ago, we dated a couple of times, but nothing came of it."

"Wow."

"Yeah, he's a playboy, and I realized that he was not the one for me."

"Hmm."

"Yeah, but the interesting thing is, when I returned from Cape Breton, he bought me flowers and supported me in team meetings and dropped by my office to chat. He then invited me out to dinner to tell me he was taking over as the sole owner."

"Uh-oh."

"Yeah. So first, I informed him that our dinner meeting was not a date, and secondly, that I wasn't interested in him. Between you and me, my heart is somewhere else."

Bree took a sip. "And, that's great to hear."

"Yeah. Well, the sudden interest was quite tempting, because my dream is to own my own publishing company one day."

Bree smiled. "Really?"

Rachel nodded. "Yes, but I want a boutique publishing firm. I want to really connect with authors and agents, and perhaps, bring out only three or four titles a year. Find the gems. Have a small team of maybe four or five people who love books and stories as I do."

"Sounds great."

"Yeah."

Bree took another drink of coffee and set her cup down.

"If you opened a business here, we could all help. Logan is an author, I took journalism for two years, and Mark is great at marketing."

Rachel grinned. "You're full of surprises, Bree. I didn't know you took journalism."

Just then the doorbell rang a few times. "Mark!" exclaimed Bree. Rachel followed her to the door, where they threw the luggage in the closet. Bree opened the door and there stood her husband with the tree. It was a fair size with a dusting of snow still on the branches.

"What do you think?" he asked, as he shook it off on the door step.

"Love it!" said Bree.

"Me, too!" chimed in Rachel.

"Oh, hi, Rachel, great to see you again."

"And you as well."

Bree grabbed the top of the tree and they carried it in together — Mark throwing off his boots on the way. There was a spot already cleared in the corner beside the couch, where Mark set it in the stand as Bree held it straight. Once it was secure, they all backed off and admired it.

"It's perfect, said Rachel.

"Okay, let's have some more coffee," said Bree, as they all moved into the kitchen and took their familiar seats.

"Is Logan coming tonight?" asked Rachel, her voice a bit high. She hoped she didn't sound as excited as she felt.

Mark gazed at her. "Yup, should be here soon."

Rachel felt her face redden, as a wonderful sensation

rippled through her heart. They would be together again any moment. She felt as giddy as a schoolgirl.

Ten minutes later, the doorbell rang and the door opened.

Mark walked into the living room and greeted his father who removed his boots. "Hey, Da."

"Hey."

Bree and Rachel were right behind Mark.

Logan faced Rachel, his eyes sparkling from the light of the fire. His smile was wide and warm. "Hi, Rachel. Great to see you again."

Rachel extended her hand, trying to control her fluttering heart. "So nice to see you again, Logan. How have you been?"

"Same old, same old." He handed his parka to Mark, revealing a burgundy sweater.

Bree embraced him. "Da!"

"What would you like to drink, Da?" asked Mark on his way to the kitchen.

"How about a beer?"

"How about an eggnog?"

"A special one?"

"Yup."

"Okay, but only one."

Mark grinned. "You got it."

Bree faced Rachel. "I'm going to open a bottle of Chardonnay. Will you join me?"

"My favourite. How did you know?"

"I didn't," replied Bree, smiling.

"I swear you two are sisters," said Logan.

Being likened to young and beautiful Bree made Rachel feel great. Rachel sat at one end of the couch and Logan settled into the far end. Bree soon handed her a glass of wine and left again.

Mark returned, handed his dad the drink and turned the radio on. *White Christmas* was playing and Rachel suddenly felt in the Christmas spirit. Manhattan, work and Nick seemed a million miles away. She was in the same room as Logan, and that was all that mattered. Bree and Mark being two of her favourite peeps, didn't hurt either.

A short time later, Mark threw another log on the fire. Bree carried in a box of decorations and placed it on the carpet. A minute later, Mark went to the basement and returned with a box of Christmas lights. Mark and Bree checked out the lights and hung them on the tree. Bree then knelt down beside the box of decorations. "Come and help me, Rachel."

Rachel came over and knelt down as Bree started removing ornaments from the box. Bree selected a couple and started to hang them. "Grab whatever strikes your fancy," she said to Rachel, who soon stood beside her picking out spots on the tree that needed to be filled.

Mark went back downstairs and returned with another box. He opened it and dropped a handful of tinsel into Logan's lap. "Once the girls are done, we get to throw tinsel on the tree."

"Nice," said Logan, gathering it.

At that moment, the news came on the radio. At the end

of the local news segment, the weather lady announced a coming snowstorm.

"Sounds like we're going to get some snow in a couple of days, said Logan.

"Maybe it won't be so bad," replied Bree, who seemed unconcerned.

Rachel noticed Logan and Mark exchanging looks, though.

A short time later, Bree and Mark brought in platters loaded with Christmas treats: fruit cake, various Christmas cookies, nuts and chocolates.

"Would anyone like some coffee or tea?" Bree asked.

"Tea for me, please," replied Logan.

"I'll have some tea, too," said Rachel.

"Coffee for me, Hon," said Mark.

A short time later, Bree served the drinks.

The radio station resumed playing holiday tunes and belted out Boney M's Christmas medley. Rachel had flashbacks of her childhood, decorating the tree and house with her family. She felt warm and cozy inside. She hadn't felt like this in many years. Even when she shopped in New York at Christmas for her co-workers and friends, she felt lonely. The City had over eight million inhabitants, and yet it was filled with lonely people just like her.

As they decorated and sang along with the radio, she caught lots of looks from Logan. Each time, they smiled at each other. They were like teens with crushes. She really wanted some alone time with him. A short time later, the tree and living room were completely decorated.

The fire crackled. "Anyone interested in supper?" asked Bree, getting up.

"I'm stuffed," replied Rachel. "Plus, I ate shortly before I took the flight."

"None for me," replied Logan.

"I can snack later," answered Mark.

"Well, that makes it easy," said Bree.

An hour later, Logan announced that he was leaving.

"We've got a big day planned tomorrow, said Mark, sitting in his recliner and looking at Rachel.

"Really? What are we going to do?"

Logan stood, walked over to the entrance and put his boots on. "It's a surprise. You'll see tomorrow."

Rachel smiled. "Oh, good. I love surprises."

Bree handed Logan his parka and embraced him. Rachel wished it was her hugging the big guy.

"Good night," he said to everyone.

"Drive safely," Rachel replied.

"I will," answered Logan, opening the door and heading out. They all waved to him from the window.

Bree turned to Rachel. "Come, let me show you your room."

Mark grabbed Rachel's suitcases and rolled them to her door. Her bedroom was right across from theirs. Bree and Rachel brought the suitcases into the room, as Rachel looked around. It was a small room with a queen-sized bed covered with a blue-and-white quilt, two night stands with lamps, a dresser with a mirror and a closet. Bree walked over to the window and opened the curtains. Rachel soon stood beside her and smiled. The partially hidden moon shone off the water. She couldn't believe she was so close to the ocean. "I love this view," she said.

"Me too," answered Bree.

Rachel yawned.

"I think you're ready for bed," said Bree, who also yawned.

"Oh, yeah." They embraced. "Thanks for everything, Bree. I really mean it."

"Anytime," Bree said, as she left and closed the door. "Good night."

"Good night."

Rachel put on her pyjamas and climbed into the sack. As she lay there, she mused about the day's events. She thought about decorating the tree and the fun night. She really felt like a member of the family. She studied the quilt. It had wonderful winter scenes in each section, including snowmen. She pulled it up around her shoulders and snuggled into it. Soon, she was off to dreamland.

7

Winter Wonderland

R achel awoke to the smell of pancakes and coffee. *Yes*! She hopped out of bed, pushed on her slippers and headed down the hallway.

"Good morning!" sang Bree and Mark.

"Morning," returned Rachel, taking her usual seat at the table beside Mark.

"How did you sleep?" asked Bree, cooking at the stove.

"Wonderful. That quilt was so warm and lovely."

"It was my grandmother's."

"Wow. Thank you."

Bree served blueberry pancakes and smiled at Rachel. "For today's adventure, we're going skating at Petrie's Lake, which is right behind Da's house. Do you own a pair of skates?"

"I do, but they're in Connecticut." She ate a few bites of her pancakes. "These are sumptuous. I love blueberries!"

Bree grinned. "We know."

"Let's go to Mayflower Mall first and pick up a pair of

skates," suggested Mark.

"Sounds, great," replied Rachel, "but I'm not that great of a skater. I only go once in a blue moon."

"That's okay, said Bree," sitting down across from her.

"Have you ever played hockey?" Mark asked.

"A couple of times in Montana, when I was a kid."

"What way do you shoot?"

"I have no idea."

"Well, Bree shoots left, so we'll get you a right handed stick, just so we have both."

She grinned. "You expect me to skate *and* play hockey?"

Mark chuckled. "We can teach you to play pretty quickly."

"Don't worry, said Bree, "I'll be with you the whole time. It'll be a blast."

Two hours later, Rachel, sat in the back of the car with her new white skates in a box. She felt butterflies as they turned up White's Lane. Was her excitement for skating or for seeing Logan again? It was both, she decided. As they made the final turn at the top of the road, she saw Logan standing outside with his stick and skates. A foot of snow covered the ground.

The visitors exited the car with all their gear and walked up to Logan. Rachel shivered, as the icy wind cut through her parka.

"How's everyone this morning?" asked Logan.

"A little bit of a headache, but otherwise fine," answered Bree.

"Good," replied Mark and Rachel.

"Great! Follow me," said Logan.

They trudged along, following a path beside the barn and headed towards the lake through the trees.

"I haven't skated in two years," said Rachel, who was right behind the leader.

"Oh, don't worry, we're not pros," said Logan over his shoulder.

"*Sure*," answered Rachel, not really believe that.

A few minutes later, they stepped onto the lake. It was massive and surrounded by trees. There were already other people skating at different sections along the edges, far away. Rachel's group sat down on a big log and laced up their skates. All wore toques and gloves. A few minutes later, Logan stood, skated around a little and then stopped in front of Rachel. He held out his hand. She looked up, smiled, took his hand and rose.

"The skates fit well," she said, as she took a few strides. She could see everyone's breath, including her own, as they spoke.

"Hey, you're a pretty good skater!" exclaimed Bree, already striding around. Soon they were all skating, laughing and enjoying themselves. Rachel felt increasingly confident the more she skated.

A few minutes later, Mark grabbed two sticks, skated over and handed Rachel one. "Try this," he said. "I'm right handed. So you hold it like this with your right hand on the lower part."

She held it just like Mark showed her. For a second she had a flashback to her youth, playing hockey on Miller's

Pond with her sister and their friends. She grinned. "Yeah, this feels right. This is how I gripped my stick as a kid."

Bree and Logan grabbed their sticks and skated over. "You look like a natural," said Bree.

"Thanks. We'll see."

Logan produced a puck from his pocket and threw it down on the ice. He smiled. "This is a soft-rubber puck. So, it won't hurt you if you get accidentally hit."

"Thanks." She was actually worried about getting hit with it, so that eased her fear. As she gazed at him for a second, she realized how thoughtful he was in everything.

Mark scooped the puck with his stick and zipped across the ice.

Bree took off in another direction, tapping her stick on the ice. Mark fired a pass to her. She took the pass, turned around and shot it towards Logan, who looked at Rachel. She took the hint and skated away.

She turned around and waited for the pass, trying to balance herself with the stick on the ice. Logan shot it to her. She was a bit slow and awkward with the stick, so the puck flew well past her and stopped about thirty feet away, towards the centre of the lake. As she skated after it, she noticed how dark it was below the surface. That was actually the water under her. *Crack.* At that moment, a loud noise travelled from right under her skates across the lake. She shrieked and turned back to Logan — terrified.

Seeing the fear on her face, he raced over. Reaching her, he put an arm around her back. "It's just the ice cracking," he said.

She wrapped her arm around him and held him tight.

He squeezed her. "Don't worry."

She looked up at him.

He gazed down. "Are you okay?"

She nodded.

"Alright, stay here, I'll get the puck." He skated off and returned. "Let's play closer to shore." They skated in, and for the rest of the time, played towards the edge of the lake. Rachel knew right then that this was the man she wanted to spend the rest of her life with. Her fear had vanished and her joy and comfort had returned.

Although they were having a blast, the icy wind was nasty and after a further half hour of skating and hockey, they skated over to the log, where Rachel noticed their boots were getting nice and cold.

Mark faced his father. "Da, you were skating great out there."

"Thanks. It's been a while."

Mark gestured to his own back. "But, *your back.*"

Logan's mouth fell open. "You're right! I didn't even think about it out there." Father and son fist-bumped.

Rachel was ecstatic to hear that.

"I'm freezing!" said Bree. "Let's go for some hot chocolate."

I love that girl! Rachel was so happy Bree spoke up. Rachel and her frozen fingers wanted to leave, but she didn't want to appear wimpy in front of these hardy Canadians. "Great idea," Rachel replied.

Ten minutes later, Logan threw his gear in the pantry and joined the group at the Toyota. He jumped in the passenger seat as the foursome drove off to New Waterford. Mark pointed out various sites along the way, as they drove through Low Point, New Victoria, and finally, entered New Waterford. Rachel enjoyed the warmth of the car as much as the conversation.

As they drove through New Victoria, Bree pointed left, down a road. "The Low Point Lighthouse is right down there."

"Maybe we can stop on the way back," suggested Mark.

Logan looked out his window to the right. "Maybe."

Bree leaned over to Rachel with gritted teeth and eyebrows raised. Rachel knew what she meant. Logan, obviously, still had emotions that surrounded the lighthouse.

After driving around New Waterford for ten minutes, and looking at various places, like where Logan grew up close to shore, and where he went to high school up by Scotchtown, they made a pit stop at Mickey D's, a popular local restaurant, where each of them grabbed a hot chocolate — Logan paying.

A few minutes later, they huddled in the warm car, chatting, and then Mark drove off, heading back towards New Victoria. As they closed in on Browns Road, Mark glanced at his father. "Da?"

"Sure," Logan replied, and Mark turned right. They drove up to the lighthouse, and parked close by. Rachel loved the big red hat that sat on the seventy foot structure. The lighthouse stood on a section of snow-covered land that pushed out into the ocean.

"Let's go!" said Bree, and they all got out and walked towards the tall building. Rachel made sure to touch it; another item crossed off her bucket list.

Carrying their cups, they walked around the lighthouse a couple of times and then stood together on the side facing the rough sea. Even though it was freezing and windy, Rachel appreciated the isolation and beauty of the lighthouse and area. No wonder Logan had picked this spot for the grand finale. It was so romantic. She wondered how often he and Carly had come here. She glanced at him. He peered out towards the horizon, perhaps remembering those exact things. Rachel was proud of him for making this step today.

Bree and Mark strolled around the lighthouse, leaving her and Logan alone.

"It's a lovely spot," said Rachel. "I remember seeing the lighthouse on the way in on my last cruise."

Logan turned towards her. "Yeah, it's nice."

She sipped her chocolate that was cooling rapidly. "Thanks for taking me skating today. I had a blast."

He smiled. "You did great."

"You don't think I'm a wimp?"

He chuckled. "No. I was terrified the first time I heard the ice cracking. Still freaks me out sometimes." He stood closer to her, sipping his drink.

She didn't know if she should go there, but took a chance. "So this is the famous lighthouse."

He glanced up at the red topper. "Yup. First time I've

been here in ages."

"It was a lovely scene."

He gazed at her. "Yes, but it was inspired by my love at the time. Carly. I couldn't deal with it after she left me."

"Bree told me a tiny bit about it."

He nodded. "It's hard for me to get past it. Like I said, I'm not good at this love thing."

She stepped closer and gazed deep into his eyes. "Maybe you just never met the right person."

He returned her intense gaze with a smile. "Maybe you're right."

She leaned into him, touching his arm.

He held her arms and lowered his head.

Her lips parted.

"Can we go, it's freezing!" shouted Bree, rounding the lighthouse.

Logan stepped back quickly.

"Oh," said Bree, smiling. "I'm sorry."

Rachel chuckled. "It's okay."

Marching around the lighthouse, Mark saw everyone looking at each other. He smiled. "Did I miss something?"

They all laughed.

Later that afternoon, the foursome sat at the kitchen table playing a game of Hearts. As Rachel played her cards, she once again felt like she was part of the family. The chats, the activities, growing closer to Bree, Mark and Logan. She felt so comfortable with them.

Her mind wandered.

8
Surprises

S haking her head, Rachel laid the phone on the table. "That was *Nick* — my boss and the owner's son. He flew in on their private jet and is at the hotel in Sydney." She rolled her eyes. "I can't believe this."

Bree locked eyes with her, knowing this was bad news for Logan. "He's *here*?"

Rachel nodded. "Yup." She faced Logan. "I have to go. I need to settle this right now."

"What's it about?" asked Mark.

"It's complicated. The owner's are stepping away from the firm and want Nick to take over and they want to make some kind of offer to me."

"Well, that sounds good," said Logan.

Rachel bit her lip. "He's also interested in me."

Logan frowned. "Oh."

"Yeah, I dated him years ago, but it didn't go anywhere. Lately, he's been pursuing me, but I have warded him off, till now."

"Why did he have to fly in? Why didn't he just call?" asked Mark.

"Good questions," answered Rachel, who was starting to feel like this was all her fault. She should not have borrowed the company jet. Nick was using that favour as a way to get close to her again.

"Yeah, I don't like it," said Bree. "Do you want me, or any of us, to go with you?"

"No, I feel like I have to address this myself."

Logan gazed at her. "Can I drive you?"

"Yes, that would be great. Thank you."

A short time later, Rachel and Logan stood at the front door. Bree hugged her tight. "Don't let Nick, or anyone, bully you into anything."

"I won't."

After saying their good-byes, Logan and Rachel climbed into the truck. Soon, they were on the highway. A few minutes passed without any words being spoken.

Logan glanced at her. "Is there any possibility that you are flying back to New York with him?"

She looked out her side window. "I doubt it, but he said there was some big offer from Vanessa, his mother."

"Sounds like she's the driving force."

She turned back to him. "Yes, very perceptive."

"Be careful, like Bree said. Looks like pressure tactics."

"I will be careful."

They closed in on the hotel. "Logan, I really enjoy your company."

"Me, too."

She laughed.

He glanced over. "I mean with you."

"I know."

He smiled. "I hope you can stay. I will miss you if you go back."

"You will?"

"Yes, of course."

"Why didn't you call me in all this time?"

"I thought you wanted me to take it slow."

"Yeah, but I didn't mean *that* slow. We only had the one FaceTime. I was hoping that you'd call me yourself."

He shook his head. "I almost called you a hundred times."

She sighed. "Why didn't you? Men are so stupid."

"Yeah, sometimes we are."

She glanced over. "Sorry, I didn't mean that."

"It's okay."

He pulled up to the hotel entrance, shut the truck off and faced her. "My feelings for you have only grown."

She gazed deep into his eyes. "I never stopped thinking about you. I just wanted to make sure that ... you're the one."

He laughed. "I can't believe it. You're a big city slicker and I'm a grubby, injured oilfield worker. You have such feelings for me?"

She smiled "Remember, I'm a country girl at heart."

"I know."

He pointed backwards with his thumb. "Why don't we turn around right now and go back to Mark's?"

"I'd love to, but I have to address this now."

"Should I wait?"

"No, go back. I will call you or Bree as soon as I can."

"Are you sure?"

"Yes."

Logan hopped out and rounded the truck. Opening the door, he held out his hand. She took it and stepped down.

He smiled. "One last thing before you go in."

"Yes?"

"I started writing again."

She grabbed him, hugging him tight! "Are you serious?!"

He wrapped his arms around her. "Yes, I think you'll like book two in the series."

She stepped back and gazed into his eyes. "Logan, I'm so proud of you!"

"Well, it was you who pushed me and inspired me." He grinned. "Can you recommend a good agent?"

She raised her eyebrows and pointed her finger at him. "You don't need an agent. I'm taking it whether Big Apple does or not." She stood on her tippy-toes and kissed him on the cheek. "I'll see you soon."

He held her. "Do you promise?"

She gazed at him with all the truth and sincerity in her, knowing how important the question was. "Yes." She then hurried off towards the entrance, looking back to wave.

As she entered the lobby, she turned her attention to Nick — fuming.

Logan touched his cheek where she'd kissed him and

climbed back into the truck. He fought the urge to follow her in and protect her from Nick. As much as he hated to, he had to be an adult and go back to Mark's and wait — the hardest thing for him to do.

Nick was waiting for her in the lobby. "What is it Nick, and how dare you follow me to Cape Breton? Are you a mad stalker now?"

Nick raised his hands in protest. "Whoa, whoa, whoa. Would I have flown here if it wasn't uber important? Mother wants to talk to you."

Rachel was stunned. "Vanessa is here?"

He pointed to the elevator. "Let's talk in my room." They took the elevator up and soon stood in his executive suite. He gestured to the couch where she took a seat, and walked over to a dresser. He grabbed his phone and appeared to text someone. He then pulled out the top drawer of the dresser and turned back to her. "How is your vacation going anyway? How's the local author?"

She pursed her lips. "I could say it's none of your business."

Nick abruptly knelt down and presented her with a small red box.

She was taken aback. "Nick, what are you doing?"

"Well, I won't see you for Christmas. This is an early present. He placed it in her hand. "Open it."

"Nick, I can't."

"Why not? We've known each other for five years. We dated. I arranged the flight to Cape Breton for you."

Staring at the box in her hand and going against her better judgment, she opened it. A huge diamond stood elegantly on an gold band. Of course, the diamond sparkled like crazy. "*Nick.*"

He smiled. His eyes hopeful. "Before you say anything, I've thought a lot about this moment and about our relationship. There's no one else I can envision leading the company with and spending the rest of my life together with. Will you marry me?"

All she could see in her mind was Logan's warm green eyes gazing at her. How he comforted her on the ice. He almost kissed her at the lighthouse. She knew she loved him. At the same time, visions of a mansion, big cars and being co-owner of Big Apple danced in her head. She was a tiny bit weak-kneed. Her eyes locked on Nick, who was turning red, waiting for her answer. "Nick, the ring is lovely, and I *did* care about you in this way, a long time ago, but ..."

His eyebrows knit together. "You do realize the offer in front of you? We would be owners together. Imagine walking into the boardroom and dealing with Aiden as the owner."

She chuckled, trying to diffuse the moment. She should have listened to Bree and Logan and not come. "Yeah, it is tempting ..."

He abruptly stood. "So, what's your answer?"

He had turned back into the petulant child that she'd witnessed at Frenchette's. She handed the box back. "I'm sorry, Nick."

Grabbing the box, he shoved it into his jacket pocket. He marched over to the dresser and picked up his phone, texting again.

What is he doing? Rachel fought the urge to storm out.

A moment later, Nick's phone rang. He took the call and put it on video. "Hi, yes, she's right here." He walked over and handed Rachel the phone.

Shocked, Rachel stood up. She was suddenly face to face with Vanessa Hoffman. The owner was in her mid-seventies with silver hair and grey-blue eyes — which were staring at her under angled eyebrows. She wore a bright red top, long gold ear rings and a scowl.

"Good afternoon, Rachel." Her voice was deep.

"Good afternoon, Vanessa."

"I was hoping this would be a celebratory call — Nicholas having bought you a fabulous engagement ring and having flown all the way to Nova Scotia to propose ..."

Rachel was starting to grasp the level of manipulation going on here. Mother and son had planned all this in minute detail. "Yes, Vanessa, I—"

"And you turned him down?"

"Well, not lightly, I—"

"You have made a huge mistake, girl."

Vanessa had hired Rachel as a junior editor while she was still in university. That was twenty years ago. The owner had always treated her well, until now. But Rachel was not going to take this. She was forty. Rachel flushed. "Hold it now."

"No, you hold it. Are you still pursuing that author, that

Logan Stewart?" Vanessa raised her voice, looking like a volcano about to blow.

Rachel assumed that she meant for the book. "Yes."

"Once you presented that book in the board room, it became *our* project, *our* property. Have Nicholas or I approved your trip to Nova Scotia to offer Stewart a contract?"

"No, I—"

"Then stop. Full stop. *We* will handle all negotiations from now on. If you continue to pursue this, there will be legal consequences."

"What are you talking about?"

"You heard me. Be careful, or it could lead to your dismissal. And it could affect your pension plan with the firm."

Rachel was shocked. She hadn't planned on losing her job, and she didn't know if Vanessa's words were just idle threats. She needed to speak with Lena. Lena's brother was an attorney and sometimes gave Rachel advice.

Vanessa continued: "And there are other changes coming to Big Apple, and soon. Big changes. I want you in my office tomorrow morning. Do I make myself clear?"

Rachel felt trapped. "Yes, Vanessa ... but how ..?"

"You will fly back immediately with Nicholas. I have called all department heads to a big meeting tomorrow."

Rachel glanced at Nick, who turned away. *Coward.* She could kick herself, *and* Nick *and* Vanessa. How had she gotten herself into this position? How had she not seen this coming? The obvious thing to do was quit, but she was not fully prepared for that. She would need access to all her funds if she was to pursue her dream, and that included her company pension. Would they play hard ball with her? It sure looked like it at the moment. She'd have to sell the condo. She had to get back to New York and get things settled asap. She thought of Logan and what she'd promised him just a short time ago. She felt like a traitor, but she had no choice. "Okay." The call ended.

A half hour later, she sat in the lobby. She checked her passport, although she probably wouldn't need it. She looked for her phone to call Bree, but couldn't find it. She panicked a bit, searching every pocket and her purse, but still couldn't locate it. Sitting in her chair and feeling defeated, her eyes welled up.

A few minutes later, she heard Nick walking towards her. She quickly wiped her tears and stood up. Two male pilots and a stewardess joined them.

"Are we ready?" Nick asked.

"Yes, sir," answered the captain. "We need to leave immediately, as a snowstorm is going to hit the northeast soon."

They walked out to the waiting taxis. The pilots took the first one, and she and Nick the second. She sat in the front.

Logan was beyond frustrated, sitting on the couch sipping a coffee. An hour had passed and still no word from Rachel.

Bree poked her head in from the kitchen. "Should I make supper?"

"May as well," replied Mark. "Are you staying, Da?"

"I guess so. Do you want to try her number again?" Logan asked Bree. She'd already tried a few times, but couldn't reach her.

Bree stood in the opening to the living room and called Rachel again. She frowned and left another message. "I'm sure she wouldn't go back to New York without telling us."

"This is so strange," commented Mark, sitting in his chair.

Logan frowned. He was trying to keep his head this time, and believe in Rachel. There's no way she would make him that promise and then break it. He needed to have patience and wisdom.

Bree addressed them: "I think I'll make some burgers and fries. How does that sound?"

"Sounds good to me," answered Mark. "I'll set the table."

"Sound good," agreed Logan.

During a very quiet supper, Bree tried to phone twice again, with no success. "I'm getting worried about her," she said.

"Yeah, me too," replied Logan.

"I think we need to relax," said Mark. "We have no real indication that anything bad has happened. Maybe she's having an intense meeting with Nick. She's a top editor at a major firm. I think she can handle herself."

Bree reached for his hand. "You're probably right, Honey."

After supper, they returned to the living room. Bree served banana bread and settled down on the love seat between Logan and Mark.

The dessert didn't make Logan feel any better, though, as each half hour without hearing from Rachel just added to his growing anxiety.

Bree cleared her throat. "Da, there's something I need to tell you."

Uh-oh, thought Logan. "What?"

"Rachel told me a bit more about Nick, when she first arrived yesterday. She told me not to say anything for now, but because of what's transpiring, I think I should tell you."

Logan leaned forward on the couch. "Go ahead."

"Well, when Rachel returned to New York last time, he bought her flowers and then invited her out to dinner."

"They had a date?"

"Yes — well, it wasn't a date per se. It was a business meal. Anyway, Nick expressed interest in her and made some big offer. But she turned him down."

Logan, rubbed his jaw. "So, what are we to think — he's trying again — he's proposing?"

Bree's eyebrows raised. "I don't know. Maybe."

"Hmm. She didn't tell me any of that on the way in. In fact, we expressed feelings for each other."

"Really?" asked Mark. "That's great!"

"Is it though?" answered Logan. "*Women* — who can understand them?"

"Hey!" said Bree.

"Sorry, Bree. Just kidding."

Logan felt tired and exasperated. It had been a long day. Actually, it had been a great day before Nick showed up.

He stood up and stretched his arms. "Well, I'm heading home. Thanks for everything, Bree. Let me know if and when she makes contact."

"I will, Da."

Logan drove home, shaking his head most of the way. "I'll never understand women," he muttered to himself. Why would Rachel leave with Nick, if she did? Maybe he still had some kind of hold over her. Maybe she secretly loved him. Logan tried to fight against these negative thoughts, but it was hard. All she had to do was tell Nick off and get a taxi back, or call Bree or himself. They would've come and gotten her. No, as far as he was concerned there was no good reason that she hadn't phoned. It smacked of weak character. It smacked of Carly.

Logan had called Carly after he'd found the note. She finally answered his call after a couple of days of trying. She told him she loved him, but couldn't live in Cape Breton. She was an Alberta girl. A Calgary girl, to be specific. And all her friends and family lived there. She invited him to come visit her, but in the end he had decided not to.

He turned up White's Lane.

In his mind, Carly's reluctance to live with him in Cape Breton meant that she didn't love him enough. How could she choose a place over a person? If *he* truly loved someone, he could live with them anywhere. But he wasn't going back to Calgary. Heck, it wasn't just himself he was concerned about. He had persuaded Mark and Bree to move down also. He was going to stay in the Cape, even if he had to live forever by himself in Low Point. He had everything he needed up there.

Well, he *thought* he had everything he needed, until Rachel showed up. She had rocked his world. And now, here he was again, with woman trouble. How did he get himself into these messes? He pulled up to the house and turned the truck to face the ocean. He shut off the engine and gazed out the window, placing his keys and phone on the seat beside him.

His thoughts turned to Mark's mom, Taylor, his first real love. He had met her at a club. He smiled. They used to dance up a storm. She'd been quite a free spirit. Too free. But she'd given him a great gift. Mark. They both loved Mark to pieces. Mark was still in some sort of contact with her, whenever she popped up — almost always in a new city. Still partying.

In hindsight, Carly was the rebound relationship. He'd heard enough chatter on those radio talk shows to know that basic psychology. Other podcasts and internet shows had also given him an education on the fairer sex. So, he'd tried to honestly look at himself. Maybe *he* was the problem. Or at least half of it. He agreed with that. His parents had abandoned him with his grandmother at two years of age. She'd raised him by herself in Low Point, New Waterford and Scotchtown. She had been a good Christian woman, although a bit strict. They attended the United Church every Sunday.

He realized that his wild side had something to do with his parents neglect of him. He started drinking and smoking around sixteen, and graduated to pot by the time he left town and joined the Air Force. Thankfully, he'd settled down, years later, working with the oil companies. They had a strict *no drugs* policy, which he was now thankful for. He still had a couple of beers now and then, but the crazy nights were far behind him.

After Carly was gone for good, he tried to enjoy life again, although it was a bit lonely on the hill. Whenever he felt depressed, he popped in to Mark and Bree's, or dropped by the shop. They were always there for him. They knew he was struggling after Carly.

So, everything was perfectly fine until Rachel showed up. And, although, he'd sworn off women, at least for a while — she'd changed all that. She was incredibly beautiful. It was hard to believe she would be interested in someone like him. Not only stunning, she was smart and caring — everything a man could possibly want. He was falling for her big time. She even forgave his big stumble at Daniel's Alehouse. She was wonderful. He'd thought about shopping for a ring, but then remembered that she wanted to take it slow. Now this. How was he supposed to process this Nick thing?

He was confused.

Was she weak? Was she weak? He couldn't help but think so. Carly had been weak. He had thought Rachel was strong, but maybe he was wrong. He shook his head for the millionth time, grabbed his keys and left the vehicle. He unlocked the door, threw his keys on the table and sat in his chair in the living room. It was freezing. He started a fire and looked out the window. He recalled Rachel's first visit. She had sat right there and looked out this window. He had gazed at her intelligent blue eyes as she'd studied the ocean. It's possible that he'd started to fall in love with her at that very moment.

He walked into the kitchen and got the stove going. He would have a nice hot cup of tea and think things through. He'd also say a prayer for Rachel. Who knew what was really happening with her and Nick. Only God knew. A part of him said to trust her. She had promised to return after all.

Mark asked Bree to try again. Still nothing.

Suddenly, Mark snapped his fingers and stood up. "Phone again," he said, as he bolted out of the room.

Bree raised her eyebrows and called again. A minute later, Mark walked into the living room holding up a phone that was lit up.

"Oh my God," said Bree.

"Yup. She muted it when we played cards. Remember? It was on the floor on the far side of the bed."

Bree phoned Logan right away, but there was no answer. She left a message.

Early the next morning, Bree turned on her laptop and discovered eight short Facebook messages from Rachel:

Lost my phone! :(
Had to fly back to NY. Sorry! <3
Big changes at work.

Job on the line.

Nick proposed. Said NO!

Did I forget my phone at your place?

Will call soon with new number. <3

What is your phone number again? <3

"Yay! Rachel's in contact!"

"Really?"

"Yes, she sent me some messages. She's in New York, or home in Connecticut. She's going to call soon."

"Wow. They must have threatened her, eh?"

"Nick proposed, but she shot him down."

"Oh, wow. Call Da and let him know."

She called him again, but there was still no answer.

Mark looked out the living room window. The storm had started.

9

Big Apple Bites

Rachel was exhausted, having barely slept. She'd finally gotten home to Stamford around eight at night and fell asleep on the couch. Before that, she'd fired off a few messages to Bree.

Early the next morning, Rachel walked into her office with two small boxes and secretly started to pack personal belongings, just in case. She was going to be ready for *anything*, including being terminated. She knew she had to move, and fast.

A half hour later, Mel entered the outer office and turned the lights on. As Rachel slid her boxes behind a cabinet, Mel stepped into her office wearing a pink pantsuit with a white top and heels.

"You're back already?" she asked.

Rachel sat down. "Yeah, not by my choice."

"Why? What happened?"

Rachel spoke in hushed tones. "Nick flew into Cape Breton and proposed, for one thing."

"*Really?*"

Rachel nodded. "Yes. I turned him down, of course, but then Vanessa got on the phone and demanded that I return, immediately. Big meeting this morning."

"Yeah, I heard."

Rachel gazed at Mel from head to toe. "Hey, what happened to your glasses? And did you get a new do?"

"Yeah, just wearing my contacts. I got them a while ago, but ..."

"You look stunning."

She smiled. "Thanks."

"And your hair looks lovely. Did you put some streaks in?"

"Yeah. Like it?"

"*Love it*! Want to get together tonight?"

"Um, actually, I'm not feeling that well. Been a bit under the weather the past few days."

"Oh, sorry. Well, maybe in a few days."

"Sure."

Rachel lowered her voice. "By the way, Vanessa said big changes are coming. Be prepared."

Mel frowned. "Yeah ... I should get to work. Got lots of typing to get done."

"Okay. Also, I might be selling my condo. Let me know if you hear of anyone looking."

Mel's eyes popped. "You're moving?"

"Don't know yet. Just keeping all my options open. Keep it under your hat."

Mel turned to leave. "Of course."

A few minutes later, Rachel's office phone rang. "Hi, Lena."

"Hey. How was Cape Breton?"

"The Dragon Lady summoned me back," she whispered.

"I heard. Can you pop over?"

"Sure. Be right there."

"Got a coffee?"

"Yep."

Rachel strolled into her office, and sat down in one of the big chairs in front of Lena's desk. "What, what?"

"Close the door."

She did and sat back down.

Lena finished typing something on her keyboard, removed her glasses, and sat back. "Well, maybe it's nothing, but I saw Mel coming out of Nick's office the other day. Her clothes were ruffled and she was adjusting her skirt. She didn't notice me and took the elevator back down."

Rachel was stunned. "Are you kidding me?"

"Nope. Wanted you to know. And, of course, you've seen her makeover?"

Rachel took a sip of coffee as she stared at Lena and started to connect the dots. "Oh my goodness. You know, now that I think about it, there have been some things, like things I told her that Nick somehow knew."

Lena nodded her head. "Vanessa has called everyone in today. Zach was already on vacation, like you. He's not impressed."

"Wow. I have to see her at nine. I'm secretly packing my personal belongings. I brought in two boxes."

Lena shook her head. "Rumours are swirling."

"Yes. By the way, can Big Apple keep my pension if I quit or for any other reason?"

"Nope. They can't touch it. Our pension sits with a third party overseeing it. Why, has she been threatening you?"

"Yes, sort of. She also said I can't pursue the Logan Stewart books. I think she's going to fire me."

"Her loss. Any firm in the city would hire you in an instant."

Rachel reached across the desk and held her hand. "Thanks, friend."

"Anytime. That's what friends are for."

"Yeah, *true* friends. Gotta go."

"Keep me posted. If you need anything, call. Otherwise, see you at ten."

"Actually, can I use your cell phone for a minute. I left mine somewhere. I need to call someone in Cape Breton and let them know I'm okay."

"Of course." Lena grabbed her phone and handed it to Rachel, who called Bree.

At nine o'clock, Rachel sat outside Vanessa Hoffman's office on the top floor. She could hear the owner's raised voice behind the closed door. Rachel imagined her with fire coming out of her mouth and smoke rising out of her nostrils. A few minutes later, a red and flustered Aiden exited and blew past her on the way to the elevator. He might have been in tears. *Well, this should be fun.*

The receptionist ushered her in.

The Dragon Lady sat behind an oversized wooden desk, caked in make-up, and decked out in a bright red blazer over a white shirt. A gaudy pearl necklace and long sparkly earrings finished off her look.

Rachel sat down.

Vanessa eye's narrowed as she stared at her. "I won't rehash things from yesterday, but suffice it to say that I consider your recent actions to be reprehensible. You can no longer keep your position as the acquisitions editor. Let me know if you are interested in staying at the firm, by working in another department, for lesser pay, or if you wish to resign." Quite satisfied with herself, she grinned and leaned back in her chair, looking like the cat who swallowed the canary. "Is it your intention to resign? I heard that you're selling your condo."

How could she possibly know that already? Rachel had only told Mel. *So that confirms it. Mel is indeed a traitor. How long has she been seeing Nick behind my back? I would have wished her well. But giving my secret plans to Nick ... to Vanessa?*

"I don't know yet," answered Rachel. She felt her face getting red and stood. "Is that all?" She needed time to bounce everything off Lena, so didn't want to tip her hand.

"Yes. And I want everyone at the ten a.m. meeting."

Rachel nodded and left. She made a point to stop by Lena's office and update her.

At ten o'clock, Rachel walked into the meeting room

that was filled with department heads and their assistants. Mel and Nick were conspicuous by their absence. The tension was palpable; fear on many faces. No one's job was safe. She sat on the same chair she'd sat on a million times. Would this be the last time? Vanessa sat at the head of the table, scowling.

After everyone had taken their seats, Vanessa cleared her throat. "Thank you all for attending and a special thanks to those who returned from an early Christmas break. I have some important announcements. First, my son, Nicholas, will be taking my place as owner and CEO, effective immediately, and will be running the day to day operations, such as he has done the past few months. I expect you to give him your full support and cooperation." Most heads nodded in agreement.

Rachel glanced at Lena, who looked back at her with raised eyebrows.

Vanessa picked up a piece of paper, read it and then put it back down. "Rachel Abrams and Aiden Gooden will be stepping down from their positions. We thank them for their years of service. The new department heads will be in place when we return in January." Gasps filled the room, but no one who still wanted a job said anything.

Eyes stared at the two who had been unceremoniously dumped. Rachel sat stoically with a thin smile etched on her face. Lena smiled at her. Her support was everything.

Vanessa shuffled in her seat. "I have one more announcement. But before I do, does anyone have anything to add?"

No one did.

Vanessa intertwined her fingers and grinned from ear to ear. "I would like to announce the engagement of my son, Nicholas Hoffman, to Melanie Young. At that moment, the couple walked into the room, Nick beaming and Mel forcing a half-smile and avoiding eye contact with Rachel.

Even though she suspected something like this, Rachel was still astonished. The couple actually looked great together. She was the perfect girl for Nick. With her good looks, curves, and big hair, she'd look great in a mini skirt, sitting in his bright-red Corvette. *Enjoy your mansion and big cars. And try not to think about what he's doing when out of town on business trips.* Rachel would have felt sorry for her, if she hadn't turned into such a Judas.

Rachel checked out Mel's hand. *Wow.* There it was. The big diamond she had turned down.

A couple of people started to clap, and then most joined Vanessa in growing applause and cheers. Everyone, except Rachel and Lena. The newly engaged couple joined Vanessa at the head of the table, still standing and smiling.

Vanessa's plan was obviously to humiliate Rachel. She took this as her cue, and rose to leave.

"Where are you going?" barked Vanessa. "This meeting is not over."

"It is for me. I quit."

Gasps filled the room again.

"And so do I!" yelled Lena, erupting from her chair and joining Rachel at the doorway.

"This is outrageous!" hollered Vanessa, grabbing her

phone. "Send security to the third floor," she bellowed into it. "We have a couple of ex-employees who need an immediate escort out."

Lena's face turned red. "You are *disgusting*, you old hag! They lay one hand on either of us and I'll sue you into oblivion."

All eyes turned to Vanessa, who looked like she'd been shot by a canon, falling back in her seat and holding her chest as if she was having a heart attack.

She looked up at her son. "Nicholas, are you going to just stand there? *Do something!*"

Lena grinned. "Yeah, do something Nick. My brother, *the attorney*, would just *love* to take you on."

Nick didn't move.

Mel started to cry.

Lena put her arm around Rachel as they marched out the door and down the hallway. "Got an extra box? I've got to grab a few possessions."

Rachel laughed. "Yeah. Are you coming over tonight for a glass of bubbly?"

"Oh, yeah!" They fist-bumped and walked to their respective offices.

10

The Blizzard

O n the afternoon of December twentieth, Mark was checking a string of Christmas lights, when his phone rang. It was a New York area code.

"Hi Mark. It's Rachel. I'm truly sorry for how things turned out, for the way I left."

"It's okay, Rachel. Bree told me you messaged and called her."

"Good. I will explain everything soon, but the main reason I called is that I'm worried about Logan."

"Da? Why?"

"Well, I know the big storm has started. I've been watching it on the news. I tried to call him a couple of times to explain why I left, but I can't get a hold of him. I then called Bree, but couldn't get a hold of her, either."

"I think she's doing laundry and charging her phone. She's in the basement."

"Oh, okay."

"Maybe Da doesn't want to talk to you right now."

"I wouldn't blame him. Have you spoken to him recently?"

"No, but he's not always tied to his phone, either." Mark walked into the living room and looked out the window. "It's been snowing most of the day. There's at least two feet out there."

"What time is it there?

"Just about 4:30. Pretty dark."

"Hmm."

"I'll try to reach him and call you back. Is this your new number?"

"Yes, thanks, Mark, and I apologize again for the way I left. I probably should have stayed and handled things better ... I actually got fired today. Everything is up in the air right now, but I'm planning to get back to Cape Breton as soon as I can."

"You lost your job?"

"Yes. I stood up to Nick and his mother. And that's the price I paid."

"Sorry to hear that. I'll get back to you soon."

"Okay."

He called his dad, but it tried to go to the answering service. However, the robotic female voice told him it was full. Mark got a bad feeling. He called again. Same thing.

Just then, Bree came up from the basement and walked through the kitchen. He turned and gazed at her.

"What's wrong?" she asked.

He explained everything. "I think I'm going to take a shot out to Da's, just to make sure he's okay."

She walked over to him and stared out the window. "Are you sure? It's getting worse. There's two feet of snow on the ground, and higher drifts."

"I'll take the ski-doo."

"The *ski-doo?* Are you crazy? Da's probably fine. Now, I'll have to worry about the both of you."

He hugged her. "Don't worry, Honey, I'll be okay. I have a bad feeling about this. Something's wrong. I have to go."

She frowned. "Okay, well go then. I'd never forgive myself if something happened to Da."

"Good. I'll get ready then. Mark took his boots, went to the basement and got dressed quickly in his snowsuit, ski mask and big mitts. He then grabbed his helmet and went back upstairs. Sneaking into the bedroom, he took his switchblade out of the night stand and put it in a zipped up pocket — just in case.

He went out the back to the shed and uncovered the yellow-and-black ski-doo, driving it into the front yard. He checked the gas level. Everything was good. When he was ready, he banged on the front door.

Bree opened it and they embraced. She shivered. "Wow, it's so cold with that wind." She looked him in the eyes. "Be safe, Mark. I'll be praying the whole time."

"Thanks, Babe. Keep your phone charged. I'll call you as soon as I'm there. And if you hear anything, call me right away."

"I will. Love you."

"Love you, too." The wind was swirling as Mark started up the ski-doo and pulled down his visor. He waved to Bree who waved out the window. He was soon on the highway, and thankfully, it was empty. The snow flurries played havoc with his sight as he picked up speed, but he made good time. Soon, he was turning right on White's Lane and heading up the hill. The snow was pristine, but he made out a couple of tire tracks.

The snowfall became a full blizzard as he drove up the twisty-turny road. Just before the last long curve he saw Da's truck to the side of the road. *What the—* It was blanketed with two inches of snow, the doors closed. The Chevy looked like it had hit a small tree just off the road and was stuck. *"Oh, God."*

Mark shut off the ski-doo and hopped off, trudging through knee-high snow to the truck. He threw open the passenger door. No Da, but blood spots on the steering wheel. "Damn." Da's phone was lying on the floor. He grabbed it. Closing the door, he walked to the front of the truck and surveyed the damage. The grill and hood were dented — the tree embedded a little. The left front tire was buried. He guessed the rear one was also.

Taking a mini-flashlight out of his arm pocket, he turned it on. He pointed it down and saw his father's footprints in the snow, heading up the road. He jumped on the snowmobile, started it up and drove around the last curve. As he slowed down, he noticed a few animal tracks beside his father's footprints and a few blood spots. *"What the hell?"*

As he approached the house, the security lights came on. He shut off the ski-doo and looked towards the small barn. Staring at him were two large dogs. No — *coyotes* — snarling and barking. Mark reached for his knife as they bolted for him. The first one knocked him backwards and tried to bite his face — crashing his teeth against the visor. Mark reached for the knife which had fallen onto the footrest. He clutched it and pressed the button, opening the blade, as the second coyote bit into his leg. He screamed, grabbed the beast and stabbed it repeatedly. The other coyote took off into the woods.

Mark rose to his feet and kicked the coyote lying in the snow, making sure it was dead. He looked down at his snowsuit, which was ripped — his thigh throbbing in pain. He trudged up to the door and walked inside, closing the door behind him. "Da! Da!" He shouted.

"In here."

A trail of blood spots went from the pantry to the coal stove. He rushed into the living room, where Da sat in his chair, holding a cloth to his nose.

Mark leaned down and put a hand on his shoulder. "Are you okay? What happened?"

"I was attempting to drive to your place, but the roads were in bad shape, so turned back. I was just stupid, trying to reach the darn phone that was ringing. When I looked back up, I smashed into a tree. I banged my nose off the steering wheel. The truck was stuck, so I walked up the road. I noticed two coyotes stalking me. One attacked and bit my hand. He held it up. I just made it inside."

Mark grabbed another cloth from the kitchen and wrapped his dad's hand. "I just ran into those damn coyotes outside. One attacked me."

"Oh, God, are you okay?"

"Yeah, I killed one and the other one ran into the woods."

"Good man!"

Mark bent down. "Any other injuries?"

"Well, I've got a killer headache. Why don't you put a fire on."

"A *fire*? Da, you're going to the hospital." He looked into his eyes. "You might have a concussion. I just have to call Bree. Everyone is worried about you."

"Who's everyone?"

"Well, Rachel is the one who alerted us to the fact you were missing."

"Rachel?"

"Yeah, she's been trying to reach you for some time."

"Hmm."

Mark smiled. "I think she likes you. I need some rope."

"In the pantry."

Mark tapped his pocket. "I got your phone."

"Yeah, I forgot it in the truck last night. It was dead when I found it this morning. Tried to charge after it thawed out ..."

"Da, you need to keep your phone with you and charged, especially living up here."

"Yeah, I guess so."

While looking around the pantry, Mark called 911 and told them to expect them at the Sydney hospital. Within a few minutes, he found the rope. He then called his wife. "Hi, Bree. I'm at Da's. He's alive, but had an accident on

White's Lane. I think he has a broken nose and maybe a concussion. I'm going to bring him to the hospital. We also got attacked by coyotes. One bit Da on the hand. One attacked me and bit my leg, but it's dead."

"Oh my God, Mark! *Coyotes*? Are you okay?"

"Yeah, in a bit of pain, but I'm going to drive us to the Regional in Sydney. Already called 911 and let them know. Call Rachel and fill her in. Love you."

"Okay, love you, too. Praying for you and Da. Please be careful."

Mark walked back to the living room. "Alright, Da, let's get you on the ski-doo."

"The *ski-doo*?"

Mark laughed. "Yup."

Wearing Logan's jacket, Rachel was lying on the couch when the phone rang. "Thank God." She grabbed it off the coffee table and sat up. "Hi, Bree."

"Are you sitting down?"

"Yes, on the couch. Why?"

"Da was in an accident."

"What? An accident?"

"Yes, he's okay, he's alive. But Mark thinks he might have a broken nose and a concussion."

"*Oh my God.*"

"There's more. They were attacked by coyotes."

"*Coyotes*? What the hell are they? Like wolves?"

"Yeah, like wolves. The ones here are big. Anyway. Da was bitten on the hand and Mark on the leg. I think Mark killed one of them."

"Oh my God! This can't be real."

"Yeah, I know. Mark went out on the ski-doo. He's now driving both of them to the hospital."

Rachel started to cry. "This is all my fault. If I hadn't left, none of this would've happened."

"It's not your fault, Rachel. It's not. Come on now. I need you."

"And I need you." Tears rolled down Rachel's cheeks. "What am I going to do?"

"We're going to pray. That's what I'm doing."

"You're right. That's what Mom would do."

"When can you return?"

"Let me check online and get right back to you."

"Okay. We love you, Rachel."

"Love you, too, Bree. What would I do without you? Keep your phone close."

"I will."

Rachel put her phone on the coffee table and paced around the condo. *I need something. Wine or coffee?* She decided on tea and put the kettle on. She took a minute in the kitchen and said a quick prayer for Logan and Mark. When was the last time she'd prayed for anyone, for anything? She pictured her mom in her mind. Her strong, compassionate hazel eyes. Rachel smiled. Mom was a prayer warrior. She was always praying. Rachel hadn't kept that legacy, that's for sure. She hadn't kept much from her small-town life at all. No, she'd become a big city girl.

She walked back into the living room. She couldn't

sit. She wished the water would hurry up. Why, oh why, did this have to happen? Was not life crazy enough for her lately? She looked up. *What are you doing, God?* At least she could blame *Him*. She paced. She paced. She had just found the man she wanted to spend the rest of her life with. Her kindred spirit. And now he's on his way to the hospital. Attacked by coyotes. *Oh my God. Coyotes.* Was it not enough that he'd been in an accident?

Realizing it could have been a lot worse, she looked up again. "Thank you, Lord," she whispered. She tapped her chin with a finger. *What to do*? *What to do*? She turned on her laptop at the kitchen table and made her tea. *I need to get a flight.*

"*Ugh!*" The first thing she noticed was news about the snowstorm and cancelled flights in the northeast. She went to the Weather Network and looked up Sydney, Nova Scotia. *Great.* Tons of snow falling tonight and tomorrow. It was going to take a couple of days to get there. *Fantastic.* The one thing she didn't have in this situation was patience. She realized the persona she'd built up in New York was useless. Rachel, the independent woman. The big acquisitions editor. The fashionista. All utterly useless right now. She wished her mother was still alive. How she missed her and Dad. They were all about character. She'd become all about appearances.

She sipped her tea. At least she had Bree and Lena. True friends. She'd call them both again shortly. She was going to do everything in her power to get back to the man she loved asap. She was going to make everything right. She was going to solve her life here and there. She returned to the couch and hugged a pillow. *God help me.*

Bree was watching out the window, when the snowmobile sped up the driveway. Opening the door, she hugged Mark tight at the entrance. *"My hero."* They kissed and she helped him out of his snowsuit. It was torn and had blood stains on it, so she threw it outside, to the side of the steps. Back inside, she looked down at his ripped jeans and saw a white bandage underneath. "How's your leg, Honey?"

"It's okay. They cleaned it and put in three stitches. But it's sore."

"How's Da?"

"Good. Slight concussion. Nose is *not* broken, thank God. Two stitches in his hand. We both had to get tetanus shots for the damn coyotes."

"Oh my God. This is so crazy."

"Yup." With Bree helping, he limped to his chair and sat down.

"Can I get you a beer or coffee?"

"Coffee, please."

Bree went to the kitchen and returned, handing him a warm cup. "I still can't believe it, Mark. *Coyotes*?"

"I know, but we've been warning about them for years now."

"So, they're keeping Da overnight?"

"Yeah. And hopefully the snow will stop soon, so I can get him. The roads will have to be plowed."

"Well, the news is better than I expected. His nose isn't

broken and only a couple stitches."

"Yeah, not so bad."

She shook her head. "Rachel freaked out when I told her about the accident and the coyotes."

"I bet. You should update her."

At seven o'clock the following evening, Lena popped over for a visit.

"Sorry for cancelling yesterday," Rachel said, as they sat on the sectional.

"I totally understand. What happened?"

"Logan got in a small accident in the snowstorm and then when he had to walk up the hill to his house, he got attacked by coyotes. I still can't believe it."

Lena hugged her.

"But there is a silver lining. Bree, his daughter-in-law phoned me back and told me his injuries are not as bad as feared. Thank God! He only has a slight concussion and two stitches in his hand."

Lena smiled. "Well, that's good news. If you think about it, guys get hurt in sports all the time. You should see some of the injuries at the Rangers games."

Rachel chuckled. "Are you still going to those hockey games?"

"Oh, yeah. I love it. Nothing like a good fight after a hard day's work."

Rachel laughed. "Oh, Lena, you're totally crazy! But you make me feel a lot better about this." She jumped up. "Coffee or champagne?"

"Well, if you're sad, coffee. But if you're happy that Logan's injuries aren't so bad, then champagne."

Rachel returned with two glasses and the bottle she had on ice.

"Yay!" shouted Lena.

Rachel popped it and poured them each a glass.

Lena raised her glass. "To Logan."

"*And* to Mark, his son — who went out on his snowmobile and got him and who was also bitten by a coyote."

"Are you kidding me?"

Rachel frowned. "Nope. He was bit in the leg and got stitches too."

"Oh my goodness. Is Cape Breton filled with wild beasts?"

Rachel laughed. "No, not really."

"Good. Anyway, you better not move there. You better stay here, close to me."

"Ha, ha. We'll see."

Lena raised her eyebrows. "So, tell me all about Logan the Canadian."

"Well, he's handsome, quiet, strong, *and* ... a writer."

"Yeah, *and*?"

"The time apart did us good. When I returned for Christmas, I realized how bad I was falling for him. When he gazes at me with his piercing green eyes from underneath those long brown bangs, my knees get weak. He's so good looking." She fanned her face with her hand.

"Ooh. You're heading into steamy romance territory."

They chuckled.

Rachel gazed at her. "I wish."

"Oh, there hasn't been any ..."

"No, not yet. I actually *dissuaded* him from moving too fast. Now I regret it."

Lena lifted her glass. They clinked and both took another big gulp.

Lena grinned. "Well, you're going to have to *persuade* him to get going. Is he your *Mr. Darcy*?"

"No, but he might be my *Captain Wentworth*."

"Ah. Nice."

"Yeah, and now, after this latest crisis, all I want to do is get back there asap. I'm trying for the twenty-third." Rachel topped up their drinks. "I love him, Lena."

"I can see that."

Rachel sighed. "When we talk about writing and books, I feel like he's an old friend. My kindred spirit. I could talk with him for hours on end."

"Okay, well we have to get you back there."

"Thanks, friend."

They both leaned forward and hugged again.

"You're welcome. Now let's talk about business before you go."

Rachel frowned. "Yes, the other crisis in my life."

Lena grinned. "But wasn't it liberating? Wasn't it nice to tell off the Dragon Lady and storm out? It was one of the most exhilarating experiences of my life."

Rachel laughed. "Lena you're a riot."

"Wasn't it, fun, though?"

"Yes, it was. It was so nice to quit and walk out. It was

liberating indeed."

Lena grinned. "Did you see Aiden's face when the old hag demoted him?"

"Oh my goodness!" said Rachel, laughing. "He finally got his."

"Yep. So, what are we going to do?"

"I've always wanted to have my own firm."

Lena smiled. "*So* interesting. Are you looking for a partner?"

"Are you kidding me?"

Lena arched her eyebrows and stared at her.

Rachel took a swig of her drink. "Okay. Where would our office be?"

"How about right here in Stamford? Wouldn't have to do the ugly commute into the City anymore. At least, not every day. I'm sure we'd have some meetings there."

"That would be Heaven."

"Yeah. You could do Acquisitions and I could do Publicity."

Rachel tapped a finger on her chin. "We could hire someone for Sales and Marketing."

Lena took a sip of her drink. "I could talk to Zach. He was steaming today."

Rachel grinned. "You think he'd join us? That would be marvellous."

"Yeah, *marvellous*."

Rachel raised her eyebrows. "Um, weren't you crushing on him, at one time."

"Yeah, and I still do. I think he's my only chance to

prevent me from becoming an old maid."

Rachel chuckled. "C'mon, Lena, you're smart and pretty. Lots of guys would love to have a girl like you."

"Where are they? Actually, I'm getting old*er*, am tall and skinny and haven't had a date in forever."

"Aw." Rachel leaned over and they hugged.

Lena gazed at her. "Zach is shy and kind of goofy, but he's also handsome and brilliant."

"Well, as co-owner, I order you to call him and invite him to a meeting."

Lena grinned. "Good idea."

11

Let's Try Again

On the evening of December twenty-third, Logan, Mark and Bree sat in the living room, enjoying tea, coffee, blueberry scones and the warmth of the fire. Christmas music played and Christmas lights twinkled.

Logan, with a bandaged hand, and Mark, sat on the couch facing Bree, who knelt on the floor, surrounded by old Christmas cards from years gone by. She'd been reading them, but stopped and looked at the men. "I still can't believe you two were attacked by coyotes. We need to be very thankful your injuries weren't far worse."

Mark softly rubbed his leg. "Yup, from now on, the only good coyote is a *dead* coyote."

"I agree," said Logan. "I used to defend them all the time, but now they're just a dangerous nuisance."

"Anyone want an eggnog?" asked Bree, rising to her feet.

"Yes, please," the men answered in unison.

Car lights in the driveway, caught Bree's attention.

Ignoring them, she smiled and grabbed the drinks. She returned and handed them out, as the doorbell rang.

"Who can that be?" asked Mark, craning his head to see out the window. All he saw was a taxi turning back onto the highway.

At that moment, Bree was already opening the door. The women embraced.

"*Oh my God*!" exclaimed Logan. "What are you doing here?"

Mark just sat in stunned silence and gazed at Bree — who grinned at him. Bree hung up Rachel's coat and strolled into the living room, waving for Rachel to come in. Rachel removed her boots and walked into the middle of the room.

"Mark, can you help me in the kitchen, please?" Bree asked.

"Sure." He rose, and quickly hugged Rachel as he passed by.

Rachel, wearing a dark-blue pantsuit with a white blouse, gazed at Logan. "I know I hurt you by leaving the way I did, but I felt I had no choice at the time. I want to tell you everything that transpired since then, and I want you to wait until the very end before saying anything."

"Okay."

"Nick proposed to me at the hotel with a giant diamond. With the offer came a life of luxury and becoming co-owner of Big Apple. I turned him down."

A smile crept onto Logan's face.

"His mother, Vanessa, then threatened my job and

pension on a phone call, right after that. So, it seemed coordinated. She demanded that I return to New York immediately. She also threatened to harm your books. So, I knew I had to return and settle things once and for all. I lost my phone in the chaos of that day, so couldn't phone you or Bree.

"Once I was back, Vanessa called me into her office, where she demoted me. I then found out that my best friend and assistant, Melanie, was the new acquisitions editor. In a subsequent meeting, with all department heads present, I was humiliated further, when Vanessa announced that Nick and Mel were engaged to be married. I quit on the spot.

"I rushed home and put my condo on the market and tried to think of everything that was in front of me. I ... I ... Rachel's eyes welled up.

Logan stood. *"Rachel."*

"And then the horrible call from Bree. You were in an accident and attacked by coyotes." She gazed at his bandaged hand and black eyes. "Are you okay? How is your hand? Is your nose sore?" She started to cry.

Logan rushed to her. "My nose is tender and my hand is sore. But, other than that, I'm fine."

She gazed up at him through moist eyes, as he wrapped his arms around her. She buried her head into his chest, pulling him even closer. "Can you forgive me for leaving that day?"

"Of course. Bree told me everything. You've done nothing wrong. That owner sounds like a witch."

Rachel chuckled. "Oh, she is. We call her the *Dragon Lady*."

"I will admit I was upset and confused that day. I knew Nick was going to try something like that. I could feel it. I was angry when hours passed without hearing from you ..."

She looked up. "I should have listened to you and Bree. It was one of the biggest mistakes of my life. You must have been so hurt."

"She really threatened to harm my books?"

Rachel sniffled. "Yes."

He gazed deep into her eyes. "Is there anything you need from me right now? Money? Anything?"

She smiled. "I need a tissue."

Bree jumped into the living room, handed Rachel a box, and left.

"Thanks, Bree. That girl is wonderful."

Logan smiled. "Yes, she is."

"I just need your understanding and support. The last thing I wanted, especially on that day, was to hurt you."

"I'm okay, especially now. There's nothing I want more on this Earth than to be with you. How did you get here? There are no flights from Halifax to Sydney in December."

"I met an older Cape Breton lady at the car rental counter in Halifax. She was renting, but was concerned with prices. We started talking and decided to rent a car together. It was incredible. Another miracle."

Logan shook his head. "*You are amazing.* You said no to Nick, quit your job, saved my books and somehow made it back in time for Christmas."

She raised a hand and softly brushed his stubbly cheek. "Does this hurt?"

"No, it feels good." He glanced at her lips and lowered his head. She stood on her tip-toes, her hands running through his hair. Her lips parted. He leaned into her as she pulled his head down, her heart racing. Their lips met. She couldn't remember what they'd been talking about. She only knew that she was in love. That he was the one. The one she wanted to be with forever. The sweet kiss lasted a long time. As her mind settled down, she realized that Logan's lips tasted extra sweet.

"Um. You taste like blueberries."

He laughed. "Bree served us scones ten minutes ago."

"Hmm." She gazed into his eyes and licked her lips. "I love blueberries."

"And I love you."

"And I love you, too."

He kissed her again.

After a minute, they stepped back from each other, still holding hands.

"I kept my promise," she said.

"You did. I will never forget."

On Christmas Eve, everyone sat in the living room wearing red-and-black pyjamas, Bree had surprised them with.

"Okay, each one of us gets to open a present," Bree announced. She grabbed one for Mark and herself and sat back down on the love seat beside him, waiting.

Rachel found one for Logan and herself and settled back down on the couch.

"Who's going first?" asked Rachel.

"Me," said Bree, giggling and ripping into her box. She soon held up a beautiful dark-blue Ralph Lauren blouse. "Wow. Thank you, Rachel."

"You're welcome. *Direct from Fifth Avenue*."

Bree continued to admire it. "I love it!"

"My turn," said Mark, who opened his big box. Searching, he finally found a small card inside. He laughed. "Thanks Da!"

"What is it?" asked Rachel.

"A Tim Hortons gift card," answered Mark.

They all chuckled.

Logan faced Rachel. "Your turn."

"This is from Bree and Mark," she said, reading the little tag, as she carefully opened the small gift, and laid the wrapping paper down. She examined the contents with a huge smile on her face, finally lifting up a pair of teal sea glass earrings.

"From *Bree's Seaglass*," announced Mark. "We saw you checking them out one day."

Rachel looked at Bree. "Did you make these?"

She nodded her head, smiling. The girls leaned over and embraced.

Rachel turned to Logan. "Your turn."

He opened the large box that sat on the floor in front of him, pulling out his old blue-and-black jacket. "Yay! You're giving it back to me?"

Rachel hopped up and walked over to the entrance area closet and removed a dark-brown leather jacket that hung on a hanger. "Would you like to trade?"

Logan stared at the new coat, which had a zipped up pocket in the left chest area. He whistled. "Wow. I love it." He stood up, as she brought it over. He slid his arms into the jacket, modelling it for all to see.

"Wow, stylin' Da!" exclaimed Mark.

"I love it," said Bree.

"Me too," replied Logan, as Rachel gave him a big hug.

He gazed at her, "For that, you get to open a gift from me."

"Really?"

He nodded.

She searched through some presents under the tree and found a small flat gift with her name on it. She pulled it out and sat down beside Logan. She shook it. "What could it be?" She unwrapped the paper and opened the box. Peeking inside, she discovered a small bronze key. She pulled it out. "What's this for?"

He grinned. "A mystery key."

She softly punched him in the arm. "Tell me!"

"Sorry, but you'll have to wait until the morning."

"It will drive me crazy."

"I know. Sorry."

She looked at Bree. "Do you know what it's for?"

"Maybe," she said coyly.

"Oh! Mark?"

"Sorry."

"That's it. No mercy from me tonight when we play Hearts."

Everyone laughed, but no one gave away the surprise.

Christmas! Awaking to the smell of pancakes, Rachel climbed out of bed and pushed into her slippers. Still wearing her Christmas pyjamas, she walked down the hallway and strolled into the kitchen. Bree was cooking and the men sat at the table. "Merry Christmas!" Rachel said.

"Merry Christmas!" they shouted in response, with hugs all around. Mark and Bree still had their pyjamas on, but Logan was dressed in his new leather coat over a black sweater and blue jeans. He looked pretty good, actually.

Rachel sat and looked at the clock. "Wow. Ten after nine. I slept in."

"You must have needed it," said Bree, placing a plate of blueberry pancakes in front of her.

Logan slid the butter and maple syrup over to Rachel with a warm smile. "Are you excited?"

"Oh, yeah! Can't wait to find out what that key is for." She took a couple of bites of her pancakes. "These taste great!"

"Thanks," replied Bree.

A short time later, Rachel was finished and the table cleared off. "Let's go open our presents," said Bree. They all headed to their favourite seats in the living room, where Bree dug out gifts for everyone. Most presents were clothing items like Christmas sweaters, toques, mitts, pants, shirts and socks. The usual fare.

Rachel then unwrapped a small box from Bree and Mark. Opening it, she found an elegant sea glass pendant. "Oh, this is lovely. It matches my earrings."

"Glad you like it!" answered Bree.

"I love it!" replied Rachel, getting up and hugging Bree and Mark.

Logan then found another gift for Rachel. "Here ya go," he said.

Sitting back down, she opened the large, flat box. Removing the box top, she discovered a pile of typed pages. The top one read: *Blueberry Kisses* by Logan Stewart.

"Eek!" She placed the box on the coffee table and dove into Logan's arms.

"Don't get too excited. It's only chapter one."

"A new romance novel?"

"Book two in the *Cape Breton Romance* series."

"Wow. I'm so proud of you, Logan. I can't wait to read it."

"Way to go, Da," said Mark.

"Oh, Da, we're so happy for you," chimed in Bree.

Rachel sat patiently while everyone opened the remaining gifts, which were mostly clothing items.

"Well, that's it," said Bree. "Who wants a coffee or tea?"

"Looks like there's one more," Rachel said, pointing to an envelope laying between two branches part way up the tree, which Bree had missed — not knowing it had been placed there early in the morning.

Bree rose and examined it. "What's this?"

"Just a little gift for you and Mark."

Bree picked it up and brought it over to Mark. She sat on the armrest. "Do you want to open it?" she asked him.

"No, you go ahead."

Bree opened it carefully and pulled out a cheque for $5,000 USD. She and Mark stared at each other and then faced Rachel. "Um, Rachel?"

Rachel reached for Logan's hand. "I spoke with Logan before I wrote it, but I wanted to help you with your back taxes and having a great start for the new year."

Bree handed the cheque to Mark. All eyes were on him.

"We can't take this," he finally said.

"Why not?" Rachel replied.

"Because, well, it's too much."

Rachel leaned forward. "Mark, and Bree, please listen to me. I knew you would have trouble accepting this, but I feel like we have become so close, like family."

"We feel the same," answered Bree.

"Yes, and I have done well for many years, and I have the funds. They're just sitting in a bank collecting interest. I want to help you. It's actually a blessing for me. After all, *it's more blessed to give than receive*, right?"

Bree and Mark gazed at each other until Mark finally broke into a smile that became a grin. "Alright then. What do you say, Bree?"

Bree jumped up. "Yes! Thank you, Rachel!"

Rachel met the couple in the middle of the room, where they embraced! Logan quickly joined them.

"Thank you so much," said Mark. "This really takes the

pressure off."

Bree turned to him. "Maybe now you won't have to go out west in the spring."

He kissed her. "Yeah, maybe I won't have to."

Later that morning, Logan faced Rachel. "Are you ready to find out what the key opens?"

"Eek! Yes!"

"Let's go, then."

"Are you guys coming?" she asked Bree and Mark.

"Nope," they replied in unison, both grinning.

Logan faced Mark. "I need your keys, Da."

Mark dug them out of his pocket and threw them to him. "Okay, Son, but no speeding."

Logan chuckled and turned to Rachel. "The truck is getting fixed. Should have it back in a week or so."

"Good." She loved that truck and wanted it back asap.

Shortly thereafter, Rachel sat beside Logan in the Toyota, passing through Whitney Pier and Sydney. Soon, they drove down Charlotte Street, the shopping district that she loved. She turned to Logan. "What have you been up to?"

He grinned. "Oh, nothing." He pulled over. "Let's see if that key fits any of these doors. Did you bring it?"

Digging into a pocket of her black leather jacket, she held it up. "Are you kidding me?"

"Let's go!" he said.

She fluttered her eyelashes. "Before we go, got any more of those blueberry kisses?"

"As many as you want." They leaned over and kissed.

She smiled. "Yummy. I want a lot."

"Me too."

They got out and walked hand-in-hand a few blocks down one side of the street. There was still lots of snow around, but the sidewalks had been cleared. She looked up. The sun was bright and warm on this blue-sky day. She chuckled to herself, as she thought of them holding hands and wearing leather jackets. They were like twenty-somethings. She snapped out of her thoughts and searched for doors to try. Logan teased her often, asking her if the key might belong to this shop or that one.

"Let's cross the street and try the other side," he suggested.

They walked for a few minutes more, her eyes darting ahead to each building, trying to figure out which door to try. As they walked past a ladies clothing store, which sidetracked her for a moment, she saw it! A shop window ahead with gold lettering:

RACHEL ABRAMS
Literary Agent

"Eek! Logan! What have you done!"

"Merry Christmas and Happy Hanukkah!" he exclaimed. They embraced.

"Merry Christmas!"

"Check it out."

She walked over to the window and peered in. The building was empty, except for a counter in the middle with a telephone sitting upon it.

"I thought I would leave the decorating to you. That is, if you like the idea. You don't have to."

"I love it!" She felt like a kid at five in the morning on Christmas day, opening the gift they wanted so bad.

"Try the key."

She walked into the narrow entrance area and stuck the key in. "Turn it with me," she said.

He reached around her and they both turned it together. *Click.* She pushed the door open and they walked in. It smelled of fresh paint and was about fifteen feet wide and forty feet in length. The walls were white and the floor made of blue tiles.

"Let's leave the door open so it airs out," said Logan.

"Good idea." She noticed a note pad and pen by the phone. "You think of everything, don't you?"

"I try, ma'am."

There was a doorway in the back of the space, so Rachel strolled over to it and peeked inside. "Ah, a little office. Perfect!"

Logan leaned on the counter. "I thought this could be a start for you. You can change anything you want. Bring in any furniture. Change any words or lettering on the window."

She hugged him again. "I love it, Logan. I have thought about this so often. It's the perfect start. The perfect gift."

Logan gazed at her. "Bree has been working on your new website."

"Are you kidding me? A website too?"

"Yup, and Mark is checking on advertising, and planning a grand opening."

She took a step back and gazed up at him, still holding

his hands. "I feel like God has given me a bigger gift this year, Logan. Bigger than all of my gifts and even this new office, which is the best Christmas present ever. *Family.*"

He smiled. "We feel the same. You're a part of our family now, and you always will be."

At that moment, a young woman with long brown hair walked into the office, followed by a middle-aged man. She smiled. "Are you open?"

Rachel chuckled. "No, sorry. This is actually my Christmas present."

"Oh, sorry. We were driving by, on the way to my Grandma's, when I saw the sign in your window."

"Are you an author?" asked Rachel.

"She's been writing stories since she was a kid," said the man, who Rachel assumed to be her father. "All her friends and family think she should be published."

Rachel glanced at Logan and addressed the aspiring writer. "Have you already looked for an agent?"

"Oh, yes. Some even asked for a full manuscript, but there's always a reason they don't like it in the end."

Rachel raised her eyebrows. "The fact that they asked for a full manuscript is a feather in your cap."

A huge grin spread across the young woman's face. "Really?"

"Yes. What's your name?"

"Amy Jones. This is my dad, Tanner."

Rachel stuck out her hand. "Pleased to meet you, Amy and Tanner. I'm Rachel Abrams and this is Logan."

Logan shook hands with the visitors.

Rachel smiled at Amy. "What genre do you write?"

"Cozy mysteries. I just finished a new one."

Rachel turned to Logan. "Do we have an email?"

"Hmm. I don't know. Maybe call Bree."

Rachel dug out her phone. "Hi Bree. Do we have an email address? I have someone at my new office who needs to send us her manuscript ... Yes, that's right."

Logan grabbed the paper and pen.

"Rachel Abrams at hot mail dot com. Thanks, Bree. And, yes, I love the new office! Talk soon."

Logan wrote it down.

Rachel folded the paper and handed it to Amy. "Send me the first three chapters of your latest novel in a PDF. How about that?"

Amy twirled. "That would be fantastic!" she said, putting the paper in her purse. "You have made my day! Merry Christmas!"

"Merry Christmas," returned Rachel, as everyone wished each other the same. Amy and her dad left, got into their truck and drove off, waving to Rachel and Logan.

"That was amazing," said Logan.

"Yes, it was. She reminds me of myself, many years ago." She reached out and took Logan's hand. "I can't wait to see what she's written. This is what got me excited when I first entered the business. How thrilling to be a young author and waiting to see what an agent thinks of your work."

"Or, even an *older* author."

"Yes, even an older author." She snuggled up to him, her head resting against his chest. "Thank you for this

wonderful gift, Logan."
He kissed the top of her head.

12

One Year Later

Rachel felt like a whale. It was the afternoon on Christmas Day, and they'd just gobbled down a delicious turkey meal that Mark had prepared. The big bird had come with stuffing, cranberry sauce, potatoes, turnip and carrots. Afterwards, in the living room, Bree served tea and coffee with blueberry pie. As they all relaxed, Rachel thought back to the morning, when Logan had opened the special gift she'd gotten him.

"Let's open our gifts!" exclaimed Bree, sitting on the armrest beside Mark.

"Who goes first?" asked Logan, sitting beside Rachel on the couch.

"Rachel!" replied Bree.

Rachel got up, found a present and sat back down. She opened it. It was a red Christmas sweater with snowmen, from Bree and Mark. She held it up. "It's wonderful. I love it!"

"You're next, Da," said Mark.

He stood, looked under the tree, and dug out a small gift. "This is from you," he said to Rachel, sitting back down.

She beamed, hoping he'd like it.

He unwrapped it. "Wow. Are you kidding me?" He held up a gold bracelet with a thick bar.

"Wow," said Mark and Bree together.

"Read the inscription," said Rachel.

"*Promise Me Forever*," replied Logan. "Sweet." He held out his arm and Rachel clasped it on. They kissed and she snuggled beside him.

"Your turn, Bree," said Rachel.

"Instead of opening a gift, we have an announcement," she replied, grinning and wrapping an arm around Mark. "We're expecting."

"Oh my goodness!" shouted Rachel, jumping up and rushing over to the couple.

Logan was on her heels, embracing everyone. "Congratulations! I can't believe it! You two will make great parents." He gazed at Rachel. "We're going to have a grandchild."

Rachel smiled. "Next Christmas is going to be extra special."

"Let's celebrate with hot chocolate," said Bree. She went to the kitchen and brought back the hot drinks a short time later.

Sipping her drink, Rachel mused on the past year. And what a year it had been. Besides the office in Sydney, she now owned a small publishing firm, Cove Island Press, with Lena in Connecticut. Logan became their first official signing. The updated and expanded *Promise Me Forever* was already a national bestseller in Canada, and had brisk sales with Barnes & Noble and Amazon in the US.

In late summer, Cove Island offered Amy Jones a contract and she and her family were over the moon. The young author was incredibly gifted and was working on two cozy mysteries.

Rachel hired Bree and Mark as part-time employees for the Sydney office, which, together with their cruise ship business, meant that Mark could stay home. Bree thanked her often for the monetary gift from last year and the new jobs. And the jobs were not charity, either, as Rachel's new staff were worth their weight in gold. Bree was the first set of eyes on new submissions, and edited manuscripts they liked. Mark did all kinds of local and national promotions and handled their social media, which really helped to spread the word. It turned out that Cape Breton was a gold mine of storytellers just waiting to be discovered.

Rachel was now splitting her time between Connecticut and the Cape, and enjoyed every minute of her new life. Lena ran the US office perfectly and they also hired a small staff. They received many excellent submissions and picked a few winners. The giant bookstore chains were in constant contact with Lena and Zach. With Lena nudging him along, he had resigned from Big Apple and become their new head of Sales and Marketing.

After Zach joined the new firm, he informed Rachel and Lena that things were falling apart at Big Apple. They'd lost most of their top executives, and Nick and his new staff were having trouble finding new books and authors. In fact, a few of their established authors contacted Cove Island about novels they were currently writing.

Big Apple meetings deteriorated often into shouting matches, and the general consensus was that Mel had no clue what she was doing. Rachel took no real joy in the destruction of Big Apple, but it did give her some satisfaction. Regardless, she was moving on.

She often thought back on her first two cruises to Cape Breton to when she'd first met Mark, Bree and Logan. She had no idea her life was going to change so dramatically. At first, she had trepidation about all the big changes, but later learned to embrace them. Logan imparted a lot of wisdom to her and was a great help in navigating new waters. He'd even visited Connecticut a couple of times. He loved it and never pressured her to move permanently to Canada. She showed him the new office, introducing him to everyone, and brought him to her favourite spots — West Beach and Cove Island.

As she thought about summer and beaches, she remembered back to August, when Logan had taken her to Dominion Beach, a short drive from South Bar. They'd walked along the sandy shore, hand-in-hand. She loved the popular spot, but it was crowded on warm days. After school began, he took her there again, on a Thursday in early September. They had the beach all to themselves. They spent half the day there, sitting on a blanket facing the sea, eating a nice lunch they'd packed and taking long strolls along the water's edge. She asked him to include the spot in his next novel.

In late summer, they'd also picked tons of blueberries in Low Point. Lots of the little berries never made it into Brees baking, though, as Rachel ate handfuls out of her bucket as they picked. She smiled, remembering how Logan caught her eating them. He'd become her best friend and rock and she couldn't be more in love.

Taking another sip of hot chocolate, she noticed Logan gazing at her.

"How about a nice drive?" he asked.

"Sounds lovely. It's so beautiful out. Where to?"

"You'll see."

A half hour later, they turned down Brown's Road towards the lighthouse.

Rachel smiled. "Ah, good choice. Haven't been here since the summer."

"Yeah."

They parked, got out and walked around the lighthouse. Standing on the snow-covered ground, they faced the ocean. It was chilly, with light fog rolling in.

She turned to face him. "This always reminds me of *Promise Me Forever*. I think I started to fall in love with you after I read that last chapter."

"And I'm so glad you did ... *Oh my goodness*!" He pointed behind her. "Why is there a cruise ship in today?"

She spun, but saw nothing but fog and the grey sea. She turned back towards Logan, who was kneeling and holding a small white box with a red ribbon.

"*Logan*," she whispered. She took the box and opened it.

Lifting the elegant ring, she examined it — a spectacular diamond on a gold band. "It's *so* beautiful."

"Rachel Abrams, will you—

"Yes!" She jumped into his arms, causing them to tumble into the snow. They kissed and then just lay on their backs, laughing.

"Don't lose the ring!" he shouted.

"Never!" she answered. They got up and Rachel handed him the box. She removed her glove, extending her arm and hand.

Logan pushed the engagement ring onto her finger. It fit perfectly.

She admired it, then gazed at him.

Gazing deep into her eyes, he wrapped his strong arms around her, grabbed the back of her coat and pulled her into a tight embrace. "You've made me the happiest man alive."

"And I'm the happiest woman."

Logan whispered in her ear: "*He gazed deep into her eyes and knew it was true. He grabbed her and they kissed again. Long and deep. They stayed in each other's arms for what seemed like forever. He had won her heart. And that was all that mattered.*"

Rachel sighed and leaned her head back. Their lips met. A minute later, she licked her lips. "You taste like ..."

He laughed. "Blueberries?"

She giggled. "No, hot chocolate."

He kissed her again.

Driving back to Mark and Bree's, Rachel debated to bring up something that was troubling her. She didn't want to wreck the wonderful moment and day, but it was intimately connected. She stared down at her sparkling ring. She totally loved it. "Logan?"

"Yes."

"Did you see the large white house for sale close to Mark and Bree's?"

"Yeah, it went on sale in November. I heard the family wants to stay out west."

"I checked it out online."

Logan glanced at her. "You don't want to live on the top of White's Lane?"

"Please don't be offended. I wanted to bring this up before, but didn't want to hurt your feelings."

"There's nothing you can't discuss with me."

She gazed out the front window. "It's kind of isolated up there. And, in winter the plows have a hard time driving to the top. And then there was the coyote attack. I still think I have PTSD from that — and it happened to you and Mark. I don't think I'm ready to live in the woods, just yet.

"I'm still a city girl at heart. Actually, I'm somewhere in between. In between the girl I was in Montana and the woman I became in New York."

He reached over and held her hand.

She turned to him. "Do you understand what I'm trying to say?"

He glanced at her. "I think so. You've had a lot of big changes in the past year, plus you're a social person, who needs people and interaction. You don't want to be stuck in a small house in the middle of nowhere."

"Yes. That's it in a nutshell." She unbuckled herself and slid next to him. Buckling herself in again, she held his hand between hers. "I want to spend the rest of my life with you."

"Well that's good, we just got engaged."

She laughed. "Could we look at the house?"

"Absolutely. I just want you to be comfortable."

Rachel was relieved. That was the only stumbling block she saw in their future together. The way Logan handled it gave her great confidence in their relationship. He could have gotten mad or upset, but didn't. This was the kind of man she needed in her life. She flashed back to volatile Nick in the restaurant that night and was glad she'd escaped that trap. *Poor Melanie.*

They closed in on South Bar. "Now, where is that place?" asked Logan.

"I think it's three or four houses past Bree's."

Logan slowed down. "There it is. They drove down the long driveway and parked right beside the *For Sale* sign."

"It's a two-level split," Rachel said.

He faced her. "Call the number."

Her eyebrows arched. "Really?"

"Yeah, but it will probably just go to an answering machine."

Rachel phoned and got prepared to leave a message, when suddenly a man answered. "Oh, hi, Merry Christmas," she greeted. "Sorry to bother you during the holidays, but my boyf ... my *fiance* and I are parked outside a property in South Bar. What? Really? Yes, we'll be right here." She hung up and gazed at Logan.

"He's coming?"

She nodded. "Yes. He said he lives in Whitney Pier and is popping over right away."

Logan smiled. "Well, let's get out and look around."

They climbed out and trudged through the snow, taking in the house and neighbourhood. Walking into the tree-lined backyard, they could almost touch the ocean.

"The yard is similar to Mark's," said Logan.

"And a big deck, too. Summers would be wonderful."

Logan pointed. "I think I can see Mark's deck from here."

She swayed from side to side. "We'd be neighbours. Wouldn't that be wonderful?"

He put an arm around her. "Sure would."

A few minutes later, they heard a vehicle approaching and met the realtor around front.

The short man climbed out of his truck and walked up to them, hand extended. "Hello, I'm John Peterson." They all shook hands.

"Nice to meet you," said Logan and Rachel in unison.

He gestured towards the house. "Well, let's have a look inside." He unlocked the front door and they strolled in, removing their boots. Stairs rose and descended from the entrance area. Climbing the steps, they stood in the furnished living room. The layout was remarkably similar to Bree's, including the all-important fireplace. Rachel pointed to it and smiled, as they followed the real estate agent around. Logan nodded.

Walking into the kitchen, Rachel noticed that the colours and appliances were rather drab, but she didn't care. She wanted to put her own stamp on the place anyway, if they decided to get it. Sliding glass doors led to the deck. She stood there, staring through the windows at the ocean. It had become so important to her. It was spiritual. It connected her to Connecticut, the lighthouse, the past, the present, everything.

They took a quick tour of the bedrooms and the downstairs. Everything seemed to be in great shape. They returned to the living room upstairs, where Rachel and Logan gazed out the main window. "I love it," she whispered to Logan.

He squeezed her hand in support.

They turned to face the agent.

"The family is looking for a quick sale," the realtor said. "They're going to get a ton of offers as soon as the holidays are over."

Rachel glanced at Logan and then spoke to the agent. "What are the options for a down payment and mortgage payments?"

He looked at his papers. "Let's see. If you could put, say, forty thousand down, it would leave you with payments of fourteen hundred monthly."

Logan raised his eyebrows and whistled. "What shape is the furnace and electrical in?"

"New furnace, hot water tank, wiring. Everything is

up to code. The family lived here for a month, but the husband got a big offer in Edmonton and they had to return immediately."

Rachel smiled. "Can we be alone for a minute?"

"Of course. I'll wait in my truck. Take your time."

"Thank you," said Logan, as the man left.

She grabbed Logan's hand. "Oh, Logan, I want this house so badly. I love the location, the proximity to the ocean, and we'd be right beside Mark and Bree."

"It's a lot of money."

"If we don't snap it up, it'll be gone soon."

"Yeah, I suppose so."

"I've got the funds," she said.

He raised his eyebrows again. "Are you sure?"

"Yes."

"Well, you could put in an offer."

"Really? You don't think I'm crazy?"

"Yeah, a little, but who isn't? Life is a risk."

She laughed.

He gazed deep into her eyes. "And I'll sell the house in Low Point. We could get the monthly payments down."

"Oh my goodness! You'd do that for me? Are you sure?"

"Of course. One hundred and ten percent."

"Oh, Logan, I couldn't be happier!" She jumped into his arms and pulled his head down, her lips pressing into his. After a minute, she leaned her head back. "I love you forever."

"Promise?"

She kissed him again.

After speaking to the very happy agent, they immediately drove to Mark and Bree's to share the incredible news.

"We're back," announced Logan, as they walked in.

Rachel put a finger to her lips. "Let's surprise them."

"C'mon in," shouted Bree. "I'm making hot chocolate."

They sat on the couch as Bree served. She returned and settled in Mark's chair.

"How was the lighthouse?" Mark asked, entering the living room and sitting on the armrest.

"Eek!" An ear-splitting shriek jolted everyone as Bree jumped up.

"What the?" questioned Mark.

"Congratulations!" shouted Bree, barely containing herself as Rachel rose to hug her.

"What is it?" asked Mark again, getting to his feet.

"Show him!" shouted Bree.

Rachel extended her hand, as Mark's mouth fell open. He hugged her tight, as Logan stood.

"Da!" exclaimed Mark, as he shook his father's hand and embraced him.

Bree gave Logan a bear hug also.

"Before you sit down, we have more exciting news," said Rachel.

Mark and Bree's eyes got big. "*More news*?" asked Bree.

"Don't worry, I'm not pregnant."

They all laughed.

"We might be buying a new house," Rachel blurted.

"Eek!" Bree screamed again.

"We might be neighbours," Logan said.

"That house?" replied Mark, pointing in the right direction.

Logan nodded. "Yup."

"Oh my goodness," squealed Bree as they all hugged again.

A minute later, Bree faced her husband. "Mark, come and help me." They left for the kitchen.

Rachel and Logan settled back on the couch.

"I feel exhausted," said Rachel, snuggling up to her love.

Yawning, he wrapped his arm around her. "Me too."

Rachel smiled as she realized he was starting to fall asleep. She lifted her hand and let the afternoon sun sparkle off her diamond. She admired it for some time.

"I don't think I've ever been happier in my life," she whispered. "*Ever.*"

Part Two

Everything For You

13
Out of the Blue

Rachel strolled along the sandy shore of Dominion Beach. It was a perfectly warm and sunny afternoon. A light breeze from the ocean washed over her. Dressed in jean cut-offs and a white summer blouse, open over a tank top, she stopped to examine a seashell. Lifting it to her ear, she listened to the sound of the ocean. She chuckled and tossed it into the sea, continuing to walk.

She loved the feel of the cool, wet sand on the soles of her feet and between her toes. Turning around, she saw Logan, wearing only long shorts, running towards her.

She laughed and jogged ahead — her hair flowing behind. She glanced over her shoulder. He was gaining on her. She giggled and kept running.

"Hey, wait up," he hollered.

She laughed and kept running.

"Rachel," he hollered.

She chuckled.

"Rachel!" she heard again, but the voice wasn't Logan's.

Looking over her shoulder, she saw Nick, dressed in a business suit and racing towards her. Fear gripped her as she ran faster.

"Rachel!" he shouted again, his voice angry.

Picking up the pace, she glanced over her shoulder again.

He gained on her.

"Get away from me!" she shouted.

Her heart pounding, she awoke and sat up. Sweat poured from her forehead.

Logan's eyes opened. "Are you okay?" he asked.

"I had a bad dream." She reached for him, laying her head on his chest.

"I thought I heard you mumbling," he said sleepily, hugging her.

"It was just a dream," she said, not wanting to tell him it was about Nick.

Logan softly stroked her hair. "It was just a dream," he repeated.

It was just a dream, she told herself over and over as she listened to Logan's steady heartbeat. After a while, she drifted off.

"Whoa, Da!"

Logan's line pulled tight. He smiled. He hadn't gone fishing with Mark in ages. They had waved good-bye to the girls this sunny morning and pushed the small aluminum boat into the water, just behind Mark's house. They drifted for a while towards Low Point and got a few nibbles right away.

Grinning, Logan thought about Rachel as he reeled in the fish. She was going to love the mackerel. The ladies had gone shopping in Sydney.

Mark pulled the line into the boat. "You've got three beauties, Da! I want to eat 'em tonight."

"Yeah, sounds good." Logan sat back and looked around, surprised to see that they were just off the lighthouse.

It instantly brought back fond memories. In this very spot he'd asked Rachel the big question last Christmas. She'd thought it the most wonderful place for a proposal, delighted that he had chosen the setting from her most favourite novel.

He smiled as a soft breeze blew through his hair.

Mark turned to face him. "I think we have our limit, Da. Should we head back?"

"Yeah, can't wait till the girls see what we caught."

Rachel and Bree strolled down a busy Charlotte Street. The June sun was glistening. Rachel wore a sleeveless white blouse and blue jeans, and Bree a pink maternity top.

Giddy and carefree, they drifted in and out of various shops and boutiques, looking at clothes for themselves and for Bree's little one.

Rachel glanced at the young woman walking next to her. Bree was in fantastic shape for being seven months pregnant. They'd already bought a selection of baby clothes, most of them in pink. Mark and Bree had found out in March that they were expecting a little girl.

Rachel smiled, recalling how Logan reacted when Bree had told them after supper one night. "We're going to have a granddaughter," he'd repeated again and again, beaming at her. He was over the moon.

Mark and Bree had wasted no time converting the spare bedroom, in which Rachel used to sleep, into their new baby room. Bree had showcased it one morning when Rachel popped over for coffee. The room contained a lovely white wicker crib. Over it dangled a cute mobile with starfish, seahorses, and a blue octopus that could light up at night. There were also two dressers, a change table, a bassinet for the first few months, and a nice old wing-back chair that Bree had designated as her nursing chair.

The bottom half of the room had been painted pale pink and the top part cream.

"Hey, shall we have a look in here?" Bree asked as they came up to another boutique.

Rachel looked into the store window. The display showed a few classy summer dresses. "Sure."

They entered and browsed through the racks with the new arrivals.

"Nice stuff," Bree said.

Rachel pulled a light-blue blouse from the rack and looked at it closely. It had beautiful linen fabric and a flattering cut.

"Do you like it?" Bree asked, glancing over to her.

"Yeah, love it."

"Try it on."

Rachel vanished into the fitting room and changed into

the blouse. A short time later, she stepped back out to show it to Bree. "What do you think?"

"*You look fabulous, darling,*" Bree said.

Rachel laughed.

Bree gazed at her. "Can I get it for you?"

"No, I'll get it," replied Rachel. She walked back to the dressing room.

"Can I see it for a second?" asked Bree as Rachel exited the room.

Rachel handed her the top, and Bree took off for the cash register.

"Hey!" hollered Rachel.

"You pay for everything," Bree shouted over her shoulder. "I'm getting this."

Rachel laughed and gave up. It was true — she was doing just that. She had to remember to let others chip in sometimes.

Bree handed her the bag as they walked outside. "Here ya go, sister."

"Why, thanks, Deary. Should we go for lunch?"

Bree smiled and rubbed her stomach. "Sounds great. We're starving." She swung her bags. "I think this girl has enough clothes for two years now."

Rachel chuckled. "What time do we have to be home?"

"I think Mark said they'll be back from fishing around two."

"Good, we have about an hour or so."

"Let's get a bite to eat then. What do you fancy?"

"What do you fancy?" replied Rachel.

They both laughed. Bree had experienced the oddest food cravings since getting pregnant. Not only pickle sandwiches, but once, she'd even dipped Cheetos in strawberry yogurt.

"I could eat a horse." Bree chuckled.

"Sounds great."

They went to Donna's Diner and sat down at a nice table by the front window. They both ordered chicken wraps, and then spent the time until the food arrived admiring their purchases.

At half past one, they were walking back to the boardwalk where Rachel had parked her car. They stopped at the crosswalk and waited for the light to change.

As they crossed the road, chatting with each other, Rachel heard an engine roaring to her right. Out of the corner of her eye, she caught a black Audi speeding towards them. She glanced at Bree, who hadn't noticed.

"Watch out!" Rachel screamed and pushed Bree towards the sidewalk.

"*What the hell*?!" Bree yelled, falling towards the curb.

At that moment, a red car pulled out from the side of the road. Tires screeched. The Audi smashed into its side. The red car catapulted towards Rachel.

She tried to jump out of the way, but it was too late. Rachel had a brief feeling of flying through the air before blacking out.

When she came to, some minutes later, Bree was kneeling beside her with tears in her eyes.

"It's okay," said Bree, softly brushing Rachel's forehead

with her fingertips. "I'm here. An ambulance is on the way."

Rachel didn't know why. She smiled at Bree and looked up at the bright blue sky. "Nick," she heard herself say.

Bree leaned closer to her. "What?"

"Nick."

"What about Nick?"

Rachel heard sirens getting louder and felt tired. She gazed at beautiful Bree.

Tears rolled down Bree's cheeks. "Hang in there, Rachel," Bree whispered to her. "I'm with you. Please, God, help us. Please help Rachel, in Jesus' name."

Rachel thought it was sweet that Bree was praying for her. God was nice. He would help them. She smiled and looked back up at the sky. It was so blue ...

The men pulled the boat onto the rocky shore just behind Mark's house, picking up the fish and gear. Arms full, they trudged up the short path.

As they approached the back deck, Mark's phone rang. "Hey —"

Logan could hear Bree's raised voice. He didn't like the look of concern in Mark's eyes. "What is it?" he asked.

Mark's brows furrowed as he ended the call and faced him. "There's been an accident."

Logan dropped the fish cooler. "An accident?"

"Car accident. They're taking Rachel to the Regional."

"How bad is —"

"I don't know, Da."

Logan waved his arm. "Let's go!"

They rushed around the house.

"I'll drive," said Mark. He took out his keys and unlocked the Toyota.

Logan jumped into the passenger seat and began to pray. Mark climbed in behind the wheel.

A short time later, they marched into Emergency.

Bree jumped up from a chair and hugged both of them. "Dr. Lemay came out to speak to me a few minutes ago. She said that Rachel has a broken leg and a head injury."

Logan shook his head. "My God. What happened?"

"We were crossing Charlotte Street ... at the intersection ... a car sped down the road. It smashed another car — a red car — and that hit Rachel."

Logan felt sick. "Oh my God."

"The driver of the car that was hit — an elderly man — was killed."

Logan shook his head.

Mark looked Bree over. "Are you okay? Your pants are ripped."

"Yeah, I scraped my knees."

"But you weren't hit?"

Bree's eyes welled up. "No, Rachel pushed me out of the way, towards the sidewalk. The doctor gave me a check-up. The baby is fine."

Logan shook his head again. "I can't believe it. Why did this have to happen? *Why?*"

Bree's eyebrows knit together. "Logan, while I knelt with her, while the ambulance was coming, Rachel whispered

Nick twice."

"*Nick*? Why?"

"I don't know. It might be nothing. I don't know. She had just been thrown through the air and hit a small tree on the sidewalk. The car that pulled out from the side of the road took most of the blow from the speeding car. That and the tree on the sidewalk saved her life."

Logan felt Mark's hand on his shoulder. "Try not to worry, Da, Rachel's going to be okay. Why don't you and Bree sit down, and I'll get us coffee."

"All right," replied Logan, trying to calm down.

A half hour later, a dark-haired woman in a white smock entered the waiting area. Her hair was in a pony tail, and she wore glasses.

Bree stood up. "Doctor Lemay, this is my husband, Mark, and this is Rachel's fiancé, Logan."

They greeted each other.

The doctor faced Logan. "Rachel has a broken right leg and a head injury including a concussion. I've ordered more tests."

Logan shook his head.

"Unfortunately, that's not all," continued the doctor. "She's in a coma."

Bree's eyes welled up. Mark put his arm around her.

Logan stared at the doctor in disbelief. "A *coma*?"

"Yes, and the sooner she comes out of it, the better."

"Can we visit her?" Mark asked.

"Tomorrow would be best. You can peek in for a minute before you leave. When you come tomorrow, talk to her, read her books and newspaper articles — tell her some good news."

"Will I be able to stay with her?" Logan asked.

"Yes, I will find out what room she'll be in. I'll let you know in a few minutes."

14
Waiting

Soft moonlight streamed through the window, highlighting Rachel's beautiful, serene face. Logan gazed at her. She looked like a porcelain doll, lying there motionless under the blue hospital blanket. A large bandage was wrapped around her head, a cast covered her lower right leg,

He yawned. The waiting was excruciating. He glanced over to the second bed in the room. Maybe he should lay down and try to sleep for a few hours. Thankfully it was unoccupied. At least they had this room to themselves while waiting and hoping. However, he felt unable to leave his post — the large brown leather chair next to Rachel's bed, which he'd hardly left during the last three days and nights. He couldn't bear to miss any sign of change, may it be ever so slight.

Logan had been busy reading to Rachel, just like Dr. Lemay recommended: newspaper articles from his iPhone as well as the texts and messages friends and colleagues had sent to them. He also brought several of her favourite books and read excerpts for her, including the last chapter of *Promise Me Forever*, all the while wishing his love would open her eyes.

He'd done additional research about people being in comas and knew it was essential that she come out of it as quickly as possible. He needed her to wake up. He was lost without her.

Rachel had been spending most of her time in Cape Breton since their engagement, and in particular, their new house, which she absolutely adored. They'd repainted and furnished it and made it their own.

The kitchen was now similar to Bree's, which was what Rachel wanted. She loved gazing at the ocean from the kitchen, and cherished sitting on the deck in the morning with a cup of tea, and, often, a blueberry scone. She'd also planted flowers all over the front and back yard.

Her favourite pastime was walking along the shoreline with Logan and sometimes discovering a new piece of sea glass. He'd also noticed that Cape Breton lingo was making its way into her vocabulary. He joked with her often that she was morphing into a Caper. She was quite happy about that.

The memories brought a smile to his face. He stood up, gave Rachel a soft kiss on the cheek and then walked over to the window and looked out. The night was clear. He could see a few stars. *Lord, please wake Rachel up. Let her know I'm here.*

After a while, he sat back down in the padded chair and

drifted off to sleep.

Awaking to a loud clatter in the hallway, Logan checked his watch. Just after seven.

He glanced over at the bed. Rachel lay unchanged and, as far as he could tell, not a hair on her head had shifted position.

He stretched his stiff legs and decided to go to the cafeteria to fetch a tea and a sandwich.

As he walked to the elevator, his phone rang. It was Detective Chiu. "Good morning."

"Hi Logan, Got time for a coffee?"

"Sure, I'm at the hospital, just heading to the cafeteria." Logan had spoken to Chiu once before on the phone, but had not met him in person. The detective had called after taking Bree's statement and asked some follow-up questions about Rachel, the accident, and her relationship to Nick Hoffman.

"I'll meet you there."

"Sounds good." Logan bought a tea and a salami-and-cheese sub and found a quiet table in a corner. He glanced around the cafeteria. Only a few people were mulling about.

He sipped his tea and had just finished his sandwich when he saw a striking six-foot tall Asian man in a blue-grey sports jacket, black tie, and dress pants enter the cafeteria.

Logan waved and the man walked over.

Chiu smiled. "Logan Stewart?"

"Yes. Nice to meet you." Logan reached out his hand.

They shook.

"Nice to meet you as well. Please, call me Jonathan." He drew out the chair opposite to Logan and sat down. Placing his Tim's coffee on the table, he pulled out a pen and a notebook and flipped through it. "I just wanted to touch base and update you on the investigation." He took a sip of his coffee.

"Sure."

"First of all, how is Rachel doing?"

"Still in a coma."

Jonathan frowned. "I'm sure she'll come out of it soon. Try not to worry."

"Thanks."

Jonathan read through his notes. "The black Audi that caused the crash was found abandoned on Pitt Street. The driver's seat was torched. Don't know if we can get any prints or DNA. Turns out it was stolen a week before the crash, which raises my suspicions. We're checking with businesses in the area to see if they caught the accident on camera. Any video would help."

Jonathan took another sip of coffee and gazed at Logan. "I did some digging into Nicholas Hoffman, based on your daughter-in-law's statement and what you told me on the phone about him. There was a Nicholas Hoffman from New York on a cruise ship that docked in Sydney two days before the accident, however he returned to the US the day before the accident. Border services confirmed that information last night."

Shivers went up Logan's back. "Nick was actually here?

That's unbelievable. How's that even possible?"

"I don't know, but I don't believe in coincidences. My American counterparts in Manhattan are assisting me on the case. We're trying to confirm all these details, and Hoffman's whereabouts. I should hear something back later today."

Exasperated, Logan shook his head. "This freaks me out. Nick must have driven that car. Rachel must have seen him. That's the only thing that makes sense. I'm going to stay by her side every second until she gets out of here."

Jonathan frowned. "I don't think we have proof that Hoffman was driving that car. Not yet anyway. We don't know what Rachel saw or what she was thinking at that moment. As far as we know right now, Hoffman was in the States on the day of the accident."

"Yeah, I suppose you're right."

Jonathan slid the notebook and pen into an inside pocket. "I've got to go, but will update you when I find out anything further. Call me when Rachel wakes up or if something comes to mind."

"I will."

Jonathan left and Logan headed back to Rachel's room. He'd call Mark and Bree soon and fill them in.

A half hour later, Logan was reading baseball scores to Rachel when an older Black man wearing a green polo t-shirt and black dress pants strolled into the room. He was of medium height and had white hair.

The man nodded and smiled. "Hi, I'm Pastor Tim from Grace Baptist Church in Sydney River. I'm just doing some visiting today and thought I might check in on you."

Logan rose to his feet and they shook hands. "Hi, I'm Logan, and this is my fiancée, Rachel." He gestured towards his love.

The pastor rubbed his well-trimmed beard and gazed at him with compassionate brown eyes. "The nurse filled me in."

"Yeah, I'm hoping and praying that she comes out of the coma soon."

The pastor nodded. "And how are you holding up?"

"Oh, I'm fine."

"Would you mind if I prayed for Rachel?"

"Not at all. Please do."

They both stepped over to the bed. Logan stood on the side closest to the chair, and the pastor walked to the other side.

Pastor Tim closed his eyes and raised his hands over Rachel.

Logan closed his eyes.

"Heavenly Father," the pastor began, his voice deep, soft and yet strong, "we come to you today in the name of your son, Jesus, and ask that you lay your healing hands upon Rachel. We ask that you would wake her up soon and that you would completely heal her head and leg. We also ask that you would comfort Logan and give him peace. You have said that we need to believe what we pray for, so we claim this healing in Jesus' mighty name. We thank you for what you are about to do, and we give you all the praise and glory, in Jesus' holy name. Amen."

"Amen," agreed Logan. He hadn't heard anyone pray like that in ages. It instantly brought back memories of his godly grandmother. He could see her sweet face and hazel eyes. She was such a woman of faith.

Pastor Tim gazed at Logan. "Now, let's leave the results to God. *Do not be afraid. Do not be dismayed.*"

Logan smiled. He knew that scripture well.

The pastor made a fist and reached over. Logan fist-bumped him.

"I've got to go," said the pastor.

Logan smiled. "Thank you so much for stopping by and praying for Rachel. It means a lot. You're welcome to come back anytime."

Pastor Tim smiled. "All right. God bless."

"And God bless you," Logan replied.

With that he was gone.

Logan just stood there, astounded at what had just happened. The man had amazing faith.

Logan straightened his shoulders. He felt as if a burden had lifted. He had the feeling that something good was going to happen. He felt peace.

15

Sunshine

The following morning, Logan grabbed a tea from the cafeteria and returned to the room. He sat in the big chair as usual, ate a blueberry muffin and read Rachel the news. Afterwards, he rose to his feet and kissed her sweet lips. He then sauntered over to the window and gazed out, sipping his tea. The sun was trying to peek out between large dark clouds. A few drops of rain pelted the window. He frowned. He was trying to be strong and keep the faith, but it was going to be another long day.

Mmm, the taste of blueberries. Rachel licked her lips. Had Logan kissed her or was she dreaming? She reminisced about their first kiss as her eyelids fluttered open. The bright lights of the room reflected off powder blue walls. She squinted. *Where am I?*

Looking down her bed, she had a start. Her right leg was in a cast. She panicked a bit, trying to remember what had happened. She noticed Logan at the window. "Hi, Honey."

Logan spun, spilling the rest of his tea. *"Oh My God*! *You're awake*!" He rushed to her side, placing his cup on the table.

"Of course, I'm awake," she replied, gazing into his eyes. "And I have the distinct taste of blueberries. Have you been kissing me?"

He grinned. "Yes, guilty as charged."

He kissed her lips. "You've been sleeping for four days."

"I have? Four days? What happened? Why is my leg in a cast?"

"You were in a car accident. What do you remember?"

"Not much, and I've got a terrible headache." She raised her hand to her forehead, discovering a large bandage.

"Let me inform the nurse you're awake. I'll be right back." Logan rushed out of the room.

"Okay, Honey." Rachel also noticed that her ring was missing. *Hmm.*

Logan returned with the nurse on his heels.

The chubby nurse stood at the foot of the bed with hands on hips. "How are you feeling, Rachel?"

"Pretty good. Can I sit up more?"

"Of course. My name is Darlene." The nurse helped her.

"Thanks. Is it possible to get a tea, Darlene?"

The nurse smiled. "You bet, Hon, be right back."

Rachel turned her head slightly. "How are Bree and Mark?"

"Doing great. In fact, I'm going to text them right now." Logan pulled out his phone.

"Oh! I remember shopping with Bree ... for baby clothes."

"That's right." Logan finished texting.

"That's it. That's all I remember."

"Excellent! You're memory is pretty good, actually. That's a great sign."

"My throat is so dry. And I'm hungry."

He grinned. "That's another good sign." He poured a cup of water at the sink in the bathroom and brought it to her.

"Thanks. Oh, that tastes good," she said as the cold liquid ran down her throat.

Nurse Darlene returned with the tea. "Dr. Lemay should be in around ten. I'm sure she'll check on you right away. Buzz or holler if you need anything, Dear."

"Am I allowed to have some food?" Rachel asked. She felt as if she hadn't eaten in a year.

"We'll have to wait until the doctor checks you over."

Rachel sipped her tea. "Okay. Thank you."

At quarter after ten, a dark-haired woman with glasses walked into the room.

"Good morning, Logan," she said.

"Good morning, Doctor."

Smiling, she turned to Rachel. "Good morning, Rachel, I am Doctor Lemay."

"Nice to meet you, Doctor. I love your French accent."

"Thank you. I recently moved from Cheticamp." She took her vital signs. "I am very happy you decided to join us. How are you feeling today?"

Rachel touched the bandage on her head. "Good, except for this headache."

"I'll examine the injury again later today. The good news is that the wound is not deep. I'll give you something for the pain. The headache should dissipate over time. We will keep you here for a while."

"Good."

"I'm going to run some tests on you over the next few days. How does your leg feel?"

"Good, although sometimes it feels a bit warm."

"That will leave over time also."

"Nice."

"Let me know if it becomes unbearable."

"Okay."

"And how is your memory? Do you remember anything from the accident?"

"Only as far as shopping with Bree, and then ... nothing."

"That's normal. Thankfully, a tree on the sidewalk broke your fall."

"Thank God," whispered Rachel.

"Yes, and you remembered Logan when you woke up?"

Rachel smiled. "Yes."

"Well, these are very good signs. I have some other patients to look in on now, but I'll pop back in to see you later again, okay?"

"Yes, thank you, Doctor."

"It is my pleasure." She smiled and left.

Logan stepped over to the bed and leaned down. "Would you like another blueberry kiss?"

"Are you kidding me?"

A short time later, Logan's phone pinged. He pulled it out of his pocket. "Detective Chiu wants to ask you a few questions about the accident. Is that okay?"

"Sure, as long as my head cooperates. From what you've told me, he sounds like a good guy."

"He is, and very professional."

Logan texted him back. "He'll be here in ten minutes."

"Okay."

Ten minutes later, the detective walked into the room.

Rising to his feet, Logan gestured towards Jonathan. "Rachel, this is Detective Chiu."

"Nice to meet you, Detective," Rachel said.

"Please call me Jonathan," he replied. "I need to ask you a few questions about the car accident, if you're up for it. If anything bothers you at any point or if you want me to stop, just say the word."

"Sure."

He pulled out his notebook and pen. "Do you remember anything about the accident?"

"No, just going in and out of shops with Bree."

"Do you remember crossing Charlotte Street?"

"No."

"Any cars?"

"No."

"Do you remember any of your conversations with Bree?"

She thought back, but still had no recollection. "There was something in a store about a blouse I liked, but no. Sorry."

Jonathan put his notebook and pen away. "That's enough for today. How are you feeling?"

Rachel touched her head bandage. "Not too bad, just this terrible headache."

He smiled. "I'll have more questions in a day or two if that is okay."

She returned a smile. "Sure. Thank you, Jonathan."

He nodded. "It's nice to see your improvement."

Rachel was surprised at how caring he was. "Thank you."

Logan walked him out.

At the elevator, Jonathan turned to him. "I'll be in touch."

"Thank you," Logan replied. "We appreciate it very much."

Logan returned to the room and sat down in the big chair.

"Is it normal for a detective to be involved with a car accident?" Rachel asked.

"I think there was a stolen car involved or something, so ..."

"Oh, I see." She looked down at her hands, which were folded together on top of the blanket. "What happened to my lovely ring?" she asked, staring at her ring finger.

He frowned. "The band is in the drawer, but the diamond is gone."

Her eyes welled up. "What happened to me, Logan?"

He rushed to her side and softly stroked her arm. "Don't think about it right now. The ring can be replaced, you can't. I'll get you another one. Don't worry about it."

She squeezed his hand. "Of course, you're right."

He kissed her cheek. "We need to take your recovery nice and slow — and be thankful for each day. It could have been much worse."

"Yes, I need to be thankful ..."

A few minutes later, Bree strolled into the room, carrying a Tim's tea and sporting a white t-shirt. "Hi, Sunshine, so glad to see you again."

"Oh, Bree, it's so lovely to see you."

Bree and Logan embraced.

She then faced Rachel. "Can I give you a hug?"

"Softly."

They hugged gently.

"How's the baby?" Rachel asked.

Bree beamed."*Penelope* is wonderful."

"Eek! You named her. I love it."

"Yeah, Mark and I made the final decision this morning. I'm sure we'll be calling her Penny."

"Oh, *Penny*. I absolutely love that name. You'll make such a great mom."

Bree smiled. "Thanks, Sweetie. Guess what? I actually brought you the proof copy of Amy's new book. I was going to read it to you. I thought you might enjoy it." She held up the hardcover.

"It looks great. I'd love to hear it."

"Are you sure you're up for it?"

"Yes, my headache is not so bad at the moment."

Bree turned to Logan. "I can stay for an hour or two if you want to get a little rest or get something done."

"That'd be great," replied Logan. He leaned down and gave Rachel a peck. "See you later, Honey."

"Bye. Love you."

"Love you, too." Logan waved to Bree and left the room.

"Have a seat," said Rachel.

Bree sat down and pulled out her phone.

Rachel closed her eyes. "I remember shopping with you, but not much after you bought me the blouse. I think my brain shut down and is not allowing me to relive the accident."

"Good brain," replied Bree. "Are you ready to hear the story?"

Rachel smiled and closed her eyes. "Oh, yeah."

"*A Writers' Group Murder* by Amy Jones."

"Ah, Amy. That girl is such a gem."

"Yes, definitely. I think this book is better than her first one. Here we go." Bree took a sip of her tea and began to read:

"Madeline Smith splashed through the pouring rain on her way to the New Horizons building in Sydney. Wearing her yellow raincoat, she felt like a child on her way to elementary school. The dark and wet October day just added to her feeling of exhilaration. She even stopped, on purpose, at a small puddle and stomped in the water with her green rubber boots. She giggled and then moved on as passers-by began to stare.

She loved Wednesday afternoon's at the seniors complex. That's when her fellow storytellers brought their latest offerings for the rest of the group to critique. And even though she was only twenty-one, she'd been able to join the group of elderly writers because last year they started to allow relatives and friends.

As Madeline ducked under the awning, just outside the doors of the building, she lowered her umbrella and shook it out. At that moment, lighting flashed across the sky a few miles away. She waited. Rumble ... rumble ... crash! Ah, how she loved a good storm. She opened the door and stepped inside.

Madeline hung up her raincoat and placed the umbrella in the bucket, already filled with fellow umbrellas, and headed into the spacious meeting room.

Her group occupied the huge round wooden table that stood in the middle of the room, surrounded by seven chairs.

Five members were already seated. There was old Mr. Quigley, wearing a blue-checkered shirt, and, beside him, his better half, Lois, dressed in a dark-green sweater. They reminded Madeline of that famous painting of the farmer and his wife (although, Madeline had recently found out it was actually his daughter).

They dutifully nodded to her. She nodded back.

Beside Lois sat voluptuous Cindy Seaver, a red-haired thirty-something, who wore a crimson top and matching lipstick. She was related to Agnes MacDonald, the facilitator.

Madeline loved Cindy's full head of hair, as her own was thin, straight, and brown. How boring. She sighed. Wasn't it bad enough that she had a boring last name? Did she have to have boring hair as well?

Beside Cindy sat Dr. Tollman, a professor of history at the university. He wore a modern navy suit with a vest, a well-trimmed grey beard, and his rather large nose held up gold-rimmed glasses. Madeline guessed that he was just shy of sixty.

Rounding out the members was the beady-eyed Mrs. Kovalchuk, a dark-haired Ukrainian widow, also close to sixty years of age — her clothes and bonnet as dark as her hair.

Madeline greeted the group cheerfully. A few hellos and gruff sounds were returned to her. She smiled and took her seat to Mr. Quigley's right, which was the same one she sat in each week — everyone taking their familiar chairs.

As strange as the make up of this group was, it was beneficial, because they each read a new portion of their latest stories each week and received critique from their fellow members.

A person needed thick skin for some of the criticisms, though, as a couple of the members took great delight in attacking the work and the author — which was hilarious, as only Dr. Tollman had been published. Actually, his cozy mystery wasn't even out yet, but he'd proudly announced a month ago that he'd been offered representation by a prestigious literary agent, who had indeed found him a large traditional publisher in Toronto. He'd read his official contract to the group two weeks ago — proudly.

Madeline would never have guessed that this was a genre he excelled in, as the excerpts he'd been reading to the group since she joined were from a science fiction novel he was working on. But Dr. Tollman's success had given Madeline confidence that she was gleaning good things from him and the other members of the group, because what Madeline desired above all things in this life was to become a published author. That was her raison d'être.

The only person missing from the table was Agnes, the seventy-something leader of the group, who was also the administrator of New Horizons.

As they all got their manuscript pages or phones ready to read, the white-haired Agnes appeared with a trolley of coffee, tea, and the usual store-bought cookies.

Madeline's chair faced the large windows that looked northeast onto the busy street. Another flash lit up the sky in the distance, followed by more rumbling. The storm was moving away. She sighed. In Madeline's mind, it was the perfect day — a storm and sharing her story.

"Hi Madeline," greeted Agnes. "Good to see you."

"And you as well."

"Come and get it," Agnes said to the group, gesturing to her trolley.

Rain pounded on the roof. The lights flickered for a moment, and the room suddenly went dark.

"Oh, no!" exclaimed Mrs. Kovalchuk.

"I hate thunderstorms," remarked Lois.

"Me too," agreed Cindy.

"Don't worry, Lois," replied her husband.

"Calm down, everyone," Dr. Tollman said. "Stay seated. Everything will be fine."

"I'm going to check the breakers," a male voice bellowed from the hallway. It was old Joe Roach, the creepy caretaker of the building. Madeline didn't like him at all, and was somewhat afraid of the tall bald man, who often wore a ratty ball cap. A couple of months before, she'd tarried behind after a meeting, and he'd accidentally locked her in. After she complained, he stared her down before finally unlocking the door. She'd noticed the smell of alcohol on his breath as she squeezed past him.

Waiting on Joe, the group patiently chatted away in the dark. Five minutes later, the lights came back on.

"Thank God," said Madeline and Lois at the same time. They chuckled.

"Thank you, Joe," Agnes hollered and turned back to the group. "Let's get our drinks and start reading."

Each member rose, grabbed a drink and cookies, and returned to their seats.

Taking her chair beside Madeline again, Agnes addressed the group. "Thank you all for coming again this week. I hope you had an inspired week and typed out many pages. Who would like to begin?"

"I would!" exclaimed Lois, beaming and shuffling her papers.

Agnes nodded.

Lois began: "My new novel is entitled Cabot Trail Mystery.*" She cleared her throat. "It was a dark and stormy night."*

Madeline chuckled inside herself as that opening line was the cliche of cliches. But she'd still listen intently to offer constructive criticism.

At that moment, Dr. Tollman grunted, gurgled and grabbed at his chest. As everyone turned their attention to him, his face smashed onto the table with a loud thud.

For a second, everyone stared in shock — then Agnes and Cindy screamed.

Mr. Quigley rose and rushed to the professor's side. He grabbed Dr. Tollman's wrist, and, after a minute, let it fall to the table. He stood stoically, staring straight ahead.

All eyes locked on Mr. Quigley's grave face as his lips moved: "I'm afraid Professor Tollman is dead."

Bree gazed at Rachel. "What do you think?"

Rachel smiled. "What an opening. As I said before, when she read us the first pages, I absolutely love it."

Bree struggled to her feet, beaming. "Me too. I couldn't wait to read the edited version to you."

"What's the final word count?"

"Sixty thousand, I believe."

"Perfect. You've done an excellent job, Bree."

"Thanks. And, of course, you can take over again when you're all better."

Rachel frowned. "That might take a while. I want you to know that I completely trust you to handle Amy. You know how I think. We're on the same page."

Bree bent down and kissed her cheek. "Thank you for that trust, Rachel. I won't let you down. Now, you just concentrate on getting better."

Rachel took her hand and smiled. "I will."

16
Mind Games

Later that afternoon, as Logan and Rachel waited for Dr. Lemay, a beaming Nurse Darlene entered the room carrying a bouquet of pink peonies in a glass vase. She placed the flowers on the bedside table. "Someone dropped them off for you downstairs at reception. Aren't they just beautiful?"

"Gorgeous," Rachel said, trying to sit up.

Circling the bed, Darlene helped her get comfortable.

Logan stepped closer to the bedside table. From between the flowers, a small white card poked out. He picked it up and stared at it:

Get well soon. N.

Shivers went up his spine. *N*! Who else could it be? It had to be Nick. He deftly moved the card to his pocket.

"Thank you, Darlene," said Rachel.

"Okay, Dear. Let me know if you need anything else." The nurse left the room.

Rachel raised her eyes from the bouquet to Logan. "Who

are they from?"

Logan faked a smile. "The card says *Get well soon*. It's not signed. Just another well-wisher. We had some flowers dropped off at the house also. Lots of Capers are wishing you a speedy recovery."

She smiled. "Capers are so thoughtful."

"I'm going to grab a coffee," said Logan. "Would you like one?"

"Could you please bring me a tea?"

"Will do. Be right back."

He walked to the waiting area and called Jonathan right away.

"Hey, Logan."

"Hey, Jonathan. Rachel just got a bouquet of flowers — card is signed *N*. I think they're from Nick."

"Don't touch the card."

"Damn. It's in my pocket. I had to hide it."

"That's okay. Don't touch it again. I'll be there shortly."

"Thanks."

Logan followed that up with a text to Mark.

Fifteen minutes later, Jonathan arrived. Logan intercepted him and walked with him to the empty waiting area.

Jonathan put a couple of small plastic bags on the table and handed him a plastic glove. "Put this on and pull the card out by the edges."

Logan did as he was instructed.

Jonathan unzipped a bag. "Drop it in."

Logan did, and Jonathan zipped it up.

"You can discard the glove," Jonathan said.

Logan removed it and tossed it into the garbage can.

Jonathan's eyebrows furrowed as he examined the card. "I take it you don't know any other folks whose name begins with an *N*.

"Nope, and it can't be another coincidence. He must be here."

"Yeah, it's weird. I'll give you that. I'll track down the flower store and find out all I can."

"Appreciated. Nurse Darlene brought them to us."

"Okay." Jonathan made some notes.

Logan thought for a minute. "I was thinking that Mark and I should guard Rachel around the clock until we find out more."

"Good idea. If it's him, he's a psychopath. He wants us to know what he's doing, that he's nearby and ready to strike again. I'll talk to the chief about getting a uniformed officer to help out."

"Thanks."

"I'm taking this to the lab right away," Jonathan said, pointing to the card. "If they can match a print to one in the Audi, it will break the case wide open." He put the notebook and pen away. "Okay, got to go."

"Thanks, Jonathan."

"You bet."

As Jonathan headed for the elevator, Mark called.

"Hey," Logan answered.

"What's up, Da?"

"Something weird just happened." Logan lowered his

voice: "Rachel got a bunch of flowers and a card from a well-wisher who signed the card with the letter N only."

"Wow. That's creepy."

"Yeah. Jonathan's all over it. I want to guard Rachel 24/7. Can you help me?"

"Of course. What time do you want me there?"

"Can you take over at five? We could do twelve on twelve off."

"Yup."

"Thanks, Son."

Laying on the couch watching the Blue Jays game, Logan grabbed another slice of his Hawaiian pizza. He'd slept for a couple of hours, but was still tired. He was trying to relax, but all he could think of was Rachel. He felt guilty even being at home, but had full trust in Mark to alert him if anything changed.

This should have been an evening of joy, after Rachel woke up from her coma, but the arrival of the flowers and the suspicious card had left him worried. The baseball game was not helping either as he couldn't care less if the Jays won or lost.

He got up and walked to the kitchen, finishing off that piece of pizza. He stopped at the sliding glass doors and stared out at the grey ocean through rain streaming down the glass. It fit his mood.

Why did these things have to happen? Was Rachel in danger or was he over-reacting? Maybe the police were right and Nick wasn't even in the country. He wanted to believe it, but he had this nagging feeling that Nick was here. Who else could the card be from? He racked his brain, but couldn't think of anyone.

His phone rang, jolting him out of his thoughts. He marched to the living room and grabbed the phone off the coffee table. It was Jonathan. "Hello?"

"Hi, Logan, do you have a few minutes?"

"Of course."

"I just heard back from my counter-part in Manhattan. He said they visited Nick's father, Ben Hoffman. Nick's mother had a stroke about a month ago. Hoffman knew that Nick had returned from a cruise recently, but had no idea where his son was now. He was uncooperative and suggested that Nick could be anywhere in the States. We're checking his residence in New York. He also owns a condo in Miami."

"Okay."

"And here's where the story gets a bit complicated. The Miami police checked out the condo building and talked to a few neighbours. Two neighbours swear they saw Nick Hoffman in the past couple of days. They saw him entering the building. They were adamant."

"I can't believe it," replied Logan.

"Yup, so that appears to be a dead end for now, but I did find out something else that's of interest. I did some digging, and it appears that a male passenger left the cruise ship, the *Zuiderdam*, in Sydney. He said he had a family emergency and had to fly back immediately to America. I don't know if that person actually left the country. I don't have a name yet because of privacy laws, but I'm getting lots of assistance from the Feds on both sides of the border. I should hear something back in the morning and will let you know as soon as I have more information."

"Okay. Thanks."

"Are you at the hospital?"

"No, Mark is there. We're doing twelve on twelve off. We haven't told Rachel anything."

"Good. I'll see if I can get a uniformed officer to help out — will run it past the Chief."

"I can't thank you enough, Jonathan."

"You don't have to, Logan. Just doing my job. Talk soon. Bye."

"Bye." Logan knew, though, that Jonathan was going above and beyond for Rachel and the family. He walked back to the couch and sat down. He shook his head. If Nick was truly in the States, and it sure looked that way now, then who had signed the card? Maybe Nick had just popped into Rachel's mind after she was hit on Charlotte Street. They say your life flashes before your eyes when you face death. Maybe numerous things went through her mind. Maybe the whole Nick thing was a red herring. He took another slice of pizza. Maybe, just maybe, things were not as bad as he thought they were.

A bell rang as Jonathan opened the door of Sweet Blossoms. The female employees were busy waiting on a couple of customers. He studied the workers: a tired-looking woman in her forties, ringing an elderly man through the cash register, and a young woman with a striped bandana tied around her blonde curls. She was busy talking to a chatty female customer while assembling an arrangement at a side table.

Within five minutes, both customers were gone. The younger lady walked over to him. Her name tag read Meg.

She smiled. "Can I help you?"

He had his wallet ready and flashed his badge. "Detective Chiu, Cape Breton Police. I'm investigating a case and need some information."

The older lady strolled over. "I'm Susie, the owner, what do you need Detective?"

"There was a bouquet of peonies delivered to the Regional yesterday afternoon. I've called and visited a few flower shops to find out who sold the flowers."

"It wasn't me," answered Susie.

"I sold a bouquet of pink peonies yesterday to a man," said Meg. "We were swamped, but I remember that."

Jonathan pulled out his notebook. "Do you recall what he looked like?"

"He was about your height. He wore a black t-shirt and a red baseball cap."

"Eye colour?"

"Couldn't see his eyes, the cap was pulled down."

"What did he say?"

"He wanted flowers for a friend at the hospital. So, I told him they need to be hypoallergenic. He asked me for suggestions. I suggested roses, carnations, and chrysanthemums, or peonies. We had some lovely pink ones, so I suggested twelve in a glass vase."

Jonathan nodded. "Yup, that's the one."

"I hope he didn't do anything bad ..."

"Sorry, I can't divulge any information. You didn't do anything wrong, so don't worry."

"He then asked for a card. I sold him one."

"Good. Do you remember anything else about him?"

"No, he seemed strange though. Like a loner or something. I didn't really pay attention."

"How did he pay?"

"Hmm." She tapped a finger on her chin. "Credit card, I believe."

"Could you find it. His name would really help."

The owner stood behind the cash screen and started typing. Meg joined her as they looked through the transactions.

Susie pointed to the screen. "Is that it?"

Meg leaned in. "Yup, that's it. William Davidson."

Jonathan wrote it down. "Can I get a copy of it?"

"Yes," said Susie. She printed it and handed it to Jonathan.

"Thank you, you have been most helpful."

"You're welcome," returned both ladies.

Jonathan was almost out the door, when he heard: "Detective!"

He turned back as Meg ran up to him.

"I just remembered. He was bald. I looked at him as he left the store. The back of his head was bald."

"Thank you, Meg, that is vital information. Please write

down everything you just told me and sign it. You might end up being a witness."

"Yes, sir."

With that, Jonathan walked to his car. He felt as if he was closing in on whoever it was, whether Nick or William. But whoever it was, they were going to deeply regret stalking Rachel.

17

Lena

Early the next morning, Rachel woke up and stared at the tall woman standing at the foot of her bed. "*Lena,* what are you doing here?"

Lena smiled. "Thought I'd come for a visit. See this *Cape Breton* you're always talking about." She stepped to the side of the bed, and they had a gentle hug. "How are you feeling?"

"I'm doing pretty good. If I could just get rid of these headaches."

"They will go in time."

"Where's Mark? Did you meet him?"

"Yes, he went for a coffee. Nice guy. Looks a lot like Logan."

"Yeah, he's a sweetie. So is Bree. Can't wait for you meet her." Rachel sat up. "I love your blouse."

Lena wore a light-green chiffon top. "Thanks. I love your new style also."

Rachel chuckled and softly touched her head bandage.

"You always make me laugh, Lena. This is my new summer collection — *cast and hat*."

"I suppose you'll want me to sign your cast?"

"Of course. I'll be saving these wonderful mementos. Where are you staying?"

"At the hotel by the cruise ship terminal."

"The Holiday Inn. You can stay at my place if you like."

"I'll wait until you're out."

"Okay. How are things with Zach?"

She smiled. "He's doing a great job."

"Nice, but how's the *friendship*?"

She sighed. "Nothing yet. I think he has a girlfriend."

Rachel frowned. "Oh, Lena."

"Yeah. As I told you, I'll die an old maid."

"Not if I have anything to do with it."

"Who wants a tall and gangly spinster?"

"With beautiful hazel eyes and a dazzling personality."

"Hmm. You always say that."

"Because it's true."

At that moment, Logan walked into the room. "Lena! So good to see you again."

"Hey, Logan."

They embraced.

Logan walked to the other side of the bed and kissed Rachel. "Mark called me. I'm just staying for a half hour."

Rachel smiled at him. "Did you get any sleep?"

"Yeah, a little. Got a pizza and watched the Jays."

"Nice."

Logan faced Lena. "Would you like a coffee or

anything?"

"Yes, that'd be lovely, and maybe a sandwich."

Logan glanced at Rachel. "If you girls are finished chatting, I can take Lena down to the cafeteria."

"Sure," replied Lena.

"Don't be long," said Rachel.

Logan gazed at Rachel. "Would you like anything?"

"Tea please."

"Okay, we'll be right back."

On the elevator, Logan faced Lena. "How are things in Connecticut?"

"Very well, thank you."

"Have you heard anything about Nick in the past couple of months?"

"I heard that Big Apple is going bankrupt."

Logan's eyebrows shot up. "Really?"

"Yep, and Mel has left Nick."

"Wow." Logan's brows furrowed. "I need to tell you something important about the accident, but we have to keep it from Rachel, for now."

Lena gave him her full attention.

"When she was lying on the sidewalk, after being struck by the car, Rachel whispered *Nick* to Bree. We don't know why. One thought, of course, is that it was Nick who tried to run her down. The Cape Breton Police are investigating. They have a detective on the case. He's already found out that Nick was actually here recently, but had returned to the US a day before the accident."

The elevator opened, and they walked towards the cafeteria.

Lena shook her head. "This is unbelievable."

"I know. It doesn't feel real. The police are working on it on both sides of the border. Some things are not adding up, so we're guarding Rachel around the clock. She doesn't remember anything about the actual accident and having mentioned Nick's name. All she remembers is shopping with Bree beforehand."

"Oh my goodness. This just freaks me right out."

Logan nodded. "Yeah, I just wanted you to know in case Rachel recalls something, or in case you see or hear anything."

"Thanks for letting me know."

Logan scanned the cafeteria for Mark, but couldn't see him. They purchased the food and drinks and returned to the fourth floor.

As they approached Rachel's room, Detective Chiu walked out.

"Hi, Logan. Just saw Rachel. She seems to be doing well. Do you have a minute?"

"Hi, Jonathan, of course." He gestured to Lena. "This is Lena Richards, Rachel's friend from Connecticut. She worked with Rachel at Big Apple Books in Manhattan, and they now have a small publishing firm together in Connecticut. She just flew in."

Logan faced Lena. "This is Detective Chiu."

"Nice to meet you," Jonathan said with a smile.

She held out her hand. "Nice to meet you as well."

He shook her hand, gazing at her. "Perhaps I could ask you a few questions later. May I have your phone number?"

"Certainly." Lena reached into her purse, pulled out a business card and handed it to him. "It's on here."

"Thank you." Jonathan slid the card into his jacket pocket.

They said good-bye and Lena strolled into Rachel's room while Logan strolled down the hallway with Jonathan.

"Do you have any news about the flowers and Nick?" Logan asked as they stood in the waiting area.

"Yes, I found the flower shop, Sweet Blossoms, and spoke to the employee who sold the bouquet. She gave me a description of the buyer: six feet tall, red ball cap, and bald. No eye colour. The US is sending me a photo soon. I checked the internet. Couldn't find much on him. Everything was scrubbed. No photographs or video. Nothing."

"Wow."

"Yeah, one more thing — William Davidson is the name of the man who bought the flowers. He paid by credit card. I've sent all that information to Detective Nichols in Manhattan."

Jonathan gazed at Logan. "Does William or Bill Davidson ring a bell?"

Logan thought for a moment. *"William Davidson*? Nope. Nothing. And the best person to talk to about Nick, besides Rachel, would be Lena. They worked with him for years."

"Yeah, I'd like to talk to her now, but I've got to run. Have a court appearance. I'll call her soon. Stay vigilant.

I don't like this case. Too many loose ends. Something doesn't add up."

With Jonathan's vast experience, Logan knew those were ominous words. After shaking hands, Jonathan took off for the stairs while Logan headed back to the room with numerous thoughts running through his head. The biggest question was, who in the world is William Davidson?

Lena strolled into the room and put Rachel's tea on the table. Mark was sitting in the chair, texting away.

"What was that?" Rachel asked, noticing Lena's red cheeks.

"Oh nothing. I just met Detective Chiu outside the door."

Rachel's eyebrows arched. "He's quite handsome."

Lena's eyes locked on Rachel's. "Yes, quite."

Butterflies. Lena sat on a bench wearing a pink short-sleeve t-shirt and white slacks as she waited for Detective Chiu at the busy boardwalk. A few fluffy clouds floated across a brilliant blue sky. Five minutes later, he emerged from a sea of tourists and walked towards her. He sported a forest-green shirt and black pants. She smiled and slid over in case he wanted to sit. He did.

"Thank you for meeting me," he said, his smokey-blue eyes warm and inviting.

"My pleasure." She tried not to stare at his chiselled facial features. Surely he had a wife or girlfriend.

He smiled. "How are you enjoying Cape Breton?"

"I love it. Haven't ventured far yet, but enjoying the

people and the scenery."

"That's good to hear. So you live and work in Connecticut?"

"Yes, in Stamford. Rachel lives close by, when she's not here. I love working with her. We're close friends."

"Nice. I was wondering if you could tell me about Nicholas Hoffman," he said, pulling out his notebook.

"Sure. He's tall. Handsome. Dresses sharply, as if he was born in an Italian designer suit. Thick, brown hair. Brown eyes. Always tanned."

"Good, that matches what I know so far. His personality?"

"Generally even-keeled, but occasionally we've seen outbursts of his wrath. Like, in the office, if there's a problem, or we miss a deadline — he raises his voice. I have witnessed him belittling staff. He likes to be in charge, but pressure seems to get to him."

Jonathan scribbled some notes.

She looked up and shook her head. "What am I saying? That's all in the past. Haven't worked with him in ages — at least a year now. But I hear things from colleagues. Big Apple is close to bankruptcy, and Melanie, his young fiancée, has left him. So... who knows?"

Jonathan cleared his throat. "It's possible that he tried to run Rachel down. Do you think he's capable of doing something like that?"

"Hard to say. I mean, I wouldn't want to accuse someone falsely."

"Right. By the way, Rachel doesn't know anything about Nick at this point ..."

"Logan told me. Don't worry, I won't say anything."

"Anything else you can add?"

"No, sorry. I hear things from Zach, a co-worker, but I don't think he knows more than that. You could talk to him, though. I have his number."

"That would be great." He pulled out his phone.

She dug hers out of her purse. "I'll put you in my contacts."

"I'll add you as well."

"Um, Detective ..?"

He smiled. "Please call me Jonathan."

She returned his smile. "Okay, Jonathan."

"And Lena is L-E-N-A?"

"Yes."

"Good." He looked up at the sky, then at the people walking on the boardwalk. "It's such a beautiful day." He sighed and glanced at the time on his phone. "I have to be in court soon."

"You must be quite busy."

"Yeah, too busy. Seems like I never have a day off."

He returned his gaze to her. Her knees got a little weak.

"Thank you for the information," he said, "very helpful."

"You're welcome."

He rose to leave.

She smiled and looked up — squinting.

He gazed down at her. "I was wondering ... if you might want to have a coffee sometime?"

A feeling of exhilaration rushed through her body. "Sure. I'd love to." *Oops. Did I answer too quickly?*

He lifted his phone and smiled. "Okay. I've got your number. I'll call you soon."

She tried to not look over-excited. "Looking forward to it."

He left. Her eyes welled up. No man had asked for her phone number in ages. *Hope springs eternal.* An image popped into her mind of a withered purple-and-yellow pansy that received a shower of rain. The flower sprang to life. She stood up and looked around. Locating the hotel, she started walking towards it. She felt like shouting and couldn't wait to tell Rachel!

A short time later, Lena stood on the ground floor of the Holiday Inn, thinking about the wonderful chat with Jonathan as she waited for the elevator.

The doors opened and a gaggle of tourists walked out.

Her eyes locked on the intense brown eyes of a tall bald man as he strolled past.

Nick! His eyes flinched for the briefest of seconds. Her heart jumped into her throat! She rushed into the elevator, turned, and punched the button for the fifth floor, keeping her eyes on his back.

He continued to walk through the foyer and did not look back. Lena's heart pounded. The elevator door closed.

Hurry! Hurry!

The doors opened. She raced to her room. Fumbling with the key card, she finally unlocked her door. Sweat poured from her forehead.

Once inside, she threw her purse on the couch and grabbed her phone. It was hard to think. She called

Jonathan's number, but only got his answering service. "*Shit.*" As she texted him, she had the impression that someone walked past her door.

She was shaking. Her fingers could barely type.

Nick at hotel!

Come quickly. Room 507

A sound outside — someone fidgeted with the door handle. She panicked, almost dropping the phone. She called Jonathan again. "Come on. Come on," she whispered. Answering machine again.

Someone knocked.

"Who is it?" she asked. No answer. She texted again.

Hurry! at door!

Her phone rang! She answered.

"I'm on the way!" Jonathan shouted.

Thank God! "The police are coming!" she yelled. "The police are coming!"

The person stopped trying the door. Silence.

"I'm at the hotel." Jonathan shouted.

He was running. Breathing deeply.

She listened to the door area intently and spoke into her phone: "He left the door area ... I think. He's bald. It was Nick. I'm certain. *Oh my God*!"

Two minutes later a loud knock on the door. "It's me," Jonathan shouted. She could hear him on the phone and through the door.

She ran to the door and flung it open. He marched in. She threw her arms around him and buried her head into his chest, shaking.

He hugged her. "It's okay. I'm here. You're okay. You're safe."

Her eyes welled up. "Thank you," she whispered. "Thank you."

"That's what I'm here for. You're okay."

He led her to the couch. For the first time, she realized he had a gun in his hand as he put it away. She felt safe. They sat. After a few minutes, she calmed down.

He called someone. "Chiu. Send two uniformed officers to the Holiday Inn immediately. Room 507. Circulate photos and wanted posters of Nicholas Hoffman. It's on my desk. Get an artist on it — one with him bald and one with hair."

Jonathan turned to Lena. "You can't remain here."

Lena sniffled. "I could stay at Rachel and Logan's place."

"Okay. I'll phone Logan and fill him in."

She nodded.

An hour later, after Mark had picked up Lena at the police station, Jonathan returned to the Holiday Inn and asked to speak with the manager. After a short while, a middle-aged woman appeared. "Yes, can I help you?"

He showed his ID. "Detective Chiu, Cape Breton Police." He pulled out a photo of Nick Hoffman. "Is this man staying at your hotel? Imagine him bald."

She picked up the photo and studied it, then called over a short male assistant. "Alex, do you know who this is? He could be bald."

Alex examined the photo. "Hmm, I'm not sure, but the

guy looks a bit like Bill Davidson. I think he's an American tourist."

Jonathan's eyebrows knit together. "When did he arrive? What room is he in?"

The manager checked the information on the reception desk's computer. "Bill Davidson checked in on the sixteenth at four in the afternoon. He's in 402."

"I need to see the room immediately," Jonathan said.

"Of course, Detective" the manager replied.

A few minutes later they were at the door of room 402.

The manager knocked. No answer. "Mr. Davidson are you here, it's housekeeping?" No answer.

Jonathan tapped her arm and showed her that he was removing his pistol.

She nodded.

He signalled for her to open the door. She did and he rushed in. They both stood in the middle of the standard room. Towels were on the floor. Drawers were open, empty.

Jonathan checked the bathroom and returned. He reholstered his gun. "He's gone."

"Yes, sure looks like it," the manager answered.

Logan felt his phone vibrating. "Give me one moment," he whispered into his phone, glancing over at the sleeping Rachel. He marched down the hallway.

"Sorry, Jonathan," he said, his voice still low. "Rachel is napping. I had to leave the room "

"Of course. I have new information from the hotel staff. They identified Nick Hoffman. He was staying at the hotel.

Checked in under the name Bill Davidson, but he's gone. I'm standing in his room right now. He left nothing behind. I have to go into headquarters to update the chief."

"My God," replied Logan.

"Yes, stay with Rachel every second."

"Will do. Mark is heading over here shortly for his shift. I'll fill him in."

"Good. How is Lena doing?"

"Very well. She's all settled at Mark and Bree's. We thought it best."

"Ah, good decision. Talk soon."

"Thanks, Jonathan."

18

A Storm Approaches

Mark rose up from the chair, stretched his legs and checked his phone. It was almost six and no new messages. Good. His head was still spinning after taking the call from his dad about Lena. It was true. Nick was actually here and stalking Rachel. In disguise. Using an alias. Attacking Lena. What a psycho. He tapped the knife in his pocket. If Nick showed up here, he was going to end up like that dead coyote.

Next to him, Rachel was still sleeping, blissfully unaware of the danger that was increasing around her. The poor woman. Why did all this have to happen? It was totally unfair. And what about Da? He'd gone through so much relationship trouble, and now he was so happy — at least until the accident. Mark loved the changes in him. Rachel and Da glowed with love and happiness. And now this. She'd just come out of the coma, and this lunatic was closing in on her.

Mark gazed at Rachel's calm face, realizing how much

he liked her. She was way more than a friend. And Bree loved her to pieces. Bree kept up a cheerful exterior, but the accident and its aftermath had shaken her. Thank God, Penny was okay. Mark shuddered. If it hadn't been for Rachel, and her brave action, Bree would have been the one in a hospital bed — or worse. He'd be forever thankful to Rachel, and he'd protect her now. It was the least he could do.

He decided to zip down to the cafeteria to fetch himself a coffee. He used the washroom first and, looking in the mirror, realized that he was wearing his camo t-shirt and ball cap. *That fits.*

Striding down the hallway, he spotted a couple of cleaning ladies in blue scrubs, standing in front of the new wanted poster. The police had quickly put them up in the hospital and all over Sydney. It showed two photos of Nick, with and without hair. The subtext read: 'Have you seen this man?'

One of the women was pointing at a photo, giggling and chatting with her friend.

What the? Mark stopped and listened.

"¿Esto es real?" the younger one asked, tapping the photo of the bald Nick with her finger.

"Seems to be," the older woman answered.

"Oh, lo siento, pensé que esto era una broma," the dark-haired one said to her colleague, shrugging her shoulders while glancing sheepishly at Mark.

"What is she saying?" asked Mark, stepping close to them.

The women turned to him.

"My friend thought it's a joke." the older one replied.

"Why?"

"Because she met the doctor yesterday."

Chills went up Mark's spine. He pointed at the photo. "You met *this* man?"

The young lady stared at the photo, squinting her eyes, and spoke Spanish again.

"What is she saying?" Mark asked.

"I'm sorry. My friend recently arrived from Chile. Her English is not so good."

"It's okay. What did she say?"

"She said he looks similar to Dr. Hall."

The younger one spoke more Spanish.

Her friend translated: "He was in the basement looking for supplies. She showed him where some things were."

"You saw *this man* here yesterday, in the basement, for certain?"

"Sí. Sí," the Chilean woman said, nodding her head.

"I need your name and phone number," Mark said to the translator. "A detective will want to talk to you. This man is not a doctor. He is very dangerous."

The woman's eyes widened. "Are you with the police?"

"No. I'm Mark Stewart. I'm related to someone who was harmed by that man."

The woman pulled out her phone from the pocket of her uniform. "My name is Sofia Gonzalez," she said. "My friend's name is Isabella Fernandez."

"Nice to meet you," returned Mark.

They exchanged numbers.

Mark bowed to both of them. "Thank you so much for your help. I've got to go." He marched back to Rachel's room, phoning Jonathan on the way. The call went to his answering service.

Mark peeked inside the room. She was still sleeping.

His phone rang. He walked down the hallway and took the call, keeping an eye on her room. "Hey, Jonathan, I have some crazy news. I just met a hospital worker who might have spotted Nick yesterday — here at the Regional, posing as a doctor."

"I'll be right there."

"Roger."

Mark immediately punched the next number. "Da, a cleaning lady might have spotted Nick at the hospital yesterday. I called Jonathan."

"I'm on the way."

Jonathan arrived a short time later. He poked his head into Rachel's room and gestured for Mark to join him. They stopped in the waiting area.

Jonathan gazed at him. "Where was the last place Hoffman was seen?"

"In the basement."

"I'm going to check it out. Stay with Rachel every second. Call me or 911 if you need to."

"Will do."

Jonathan took the elevator to the basement and began his search for Nick. He thoroughly checked the cafeteria and the Mental Health ward, but nothing seemed out of the ordinary. He continued down the hallway towards the storage rooms. That end of the hall was dimly lit, quiet, and eerie. He removed his pistol. Looking up, he noticed that a ceiling light was out — broken. *Hmm.* He poked his head into each room. As he stood outside a room he'd just checked, he heard a noise from behind. He turned, but it was far too late. A thousand stars flashed through his vision as he collapsed to the floor.

As Logan walked into the room, Rachel stirred and woke up.

"Oh, hi Honey," she said.

"Hey," returned Logan. "How are you feeling?"

She smiled. "Fine. Just had a good sleep."

He bent over and gave her a quick kiss. "I need to talk to Mark for a minute." He turned to his son. "Let's go outside."

Mark smiled at Rachel and headed for the door. "Sure, Da."

"Hey, what's going on?" asked Rachel, raising herself up in the bed. "You just came in and now you're leaving again?" Her voice had a hint of playfulness, but Logan could detect the worry underneath it.

"I'll be back soon," answered Logan.

Father and son walked down the hallway.

Logan turned to Mark. "What's going on? Is Jonathan here?"

Mark stared at his dad. "He went to the basement to

check things ten minutes ago. Haven't heard anything since. Don't want to call as he might not want his phone to ring."

"Good thinking." Logan's eyebrows knit together. "I don't like it. You stay here. I'm going to the basement."

Mark frowned. "Are you sure that's a good idea, Da?"

"No, but we've got to do something. Don't leave Rachel alone whatever you do."

"I won't. Be careful, Da."

"I will. Got your knife?"

"Yup. Got yours?"

He tapped his pocket. "Yup. Say a little prayer for me."

"Will do."

Rachel sat upright, trying to adjust the pillows behind her back. Her mind was racing. Something wasn't right. The tension was palpable. Mark was acting weird. Logan looked strained. He was concerned about something. And why were they sitting with her every second of the day? Of course, it was nice to wake up and see a familiar face, but ... She mangled a pillow with both hands. What could be the problem? She also thought about Bree. *Hmm.* Were they all keeping something from her?

At that moment, Mark walked in, no Logan though. He smiled, but it looked forced. What was he hiding?

"Sorry, it took so long," he said. "Can I get you something? Do you want a tea or —"

"What's going on, Mark? Where has Logan gone?" Her voice sounded a little shriller than she would have liked, but she didn't care. "Is everything okay?"

Mark's smile vanished. He stared at her intently. "Rachel, there's something I need to tell you."

Stepping out of the elevator, Logan looked around. The hallway was empty. He walked slowly down the corridor, stopping to search each room.

A worker in a white coat popped out of a room, scaring him half to death.

"Oh, sorry," she said, hurrying past and taking the elevator back up.

Logan continued on, searching room after room. *Where is Jonathan?* He peeked into one room, which seemed to be a storage area with bags piled up.

He stepped inside and removed the knife from his pocket. *Click.* The blade appeared. Hearing a muffled sound, he kicked a couple of blankets aside that were piled on the floor. There was something ... He moved another blanket, revealing a shoe ... black pants.

Jonathan!

At that instant, a muzzle pressed into his side.

"Well, hello, Logan Stewart. We finally meet."

Logan kept his eyes straight ahead, but out of the corner of his right eye, he could make out the eerie bald head of Nick. Fear gripped Logan, but he tried not to show it. "Yeah, we do."

"Please, throw your knife down."

Logan did.

Nick chuckled. "I think this is the climax to this romantic

thriller. How do you think this story is going to end?"

Scenarios raced through Logan's mind. His eyes darted around the room. "I don't know ... hopefully good for me."

Nick laughed and pushed the gun deeper into Logan's ribs. "You have a vivid imagination."

"I guess that makes sense, seeing how I'm an author ... Logan whacked the arm holding the gun and bolted out of the room. He raced down the hallway. *Blam*! A loud shot rang out! He looked down. Blood gushed out of his side. *Oh My God, I'm hit*. It was surreal. He dove into the nearest room and slammed the door shut. He lay on the floor, his back against the door, looking up towards the frosted window — his stomach burning, the pain intense. *God help me.*

Seconds later, the door handle moved violently — Nick trying to force the door. Logan pushed back with all his remaining strength, his heart pounding.

At that moment — voices! People exiting the elevator, walking towards them.

"The police have a suspect in a storage room!" Nick shouted. "Shots fired. Take cover!"

Boots pounded the ground. Scrambling noises. Silence. Logan heard the elevator open and close. Nick going up. He texted Mark as sweat poured from his forehead.

Nick coming. Watch out!

Still dressed in blue scrubs, Nick exited the elevator on the fourth floor. He felt ecstatic.

A nurse walked past.

He gave her a nod and a smile.

She returned his greeting.

As he walked on, he saw himself reflected in the glass of a watercolour picture. He grinned and came closer. How well he looked in this outfit. The surgical cap was a nice addition, covering most of his bald head. He missed his thick dark hair. As soon as the job was done, he'd grow it out again.

He stopped at the far end of the hallway, lit a match and dropped it into a garbage container. After a moment, smoke started to rise. He waited, smiled and tipped over the can. He waited some more. It was catching nicely. He then looked for the fire alarm and pulled it. "Fire!" he yelled. "Fire!"

Immediately, the floor sprang to life as medical staff raced down hallways and removed patients. He glanced back. The fire grew. The alarm rang in his ears. He grinned and walked towards Rachel's room, humming *Happy Days Are Here Again*.

Strolling past her room, he looked in. Rachel was lying under the covers in her bed, but no police or medical presence. Perfect. He continued down that end of the hallway as staff and patients motored by, heading to elevators and stairs. He lit another match and dropped it into another garbage bin. A minute later, flames and smoke billowed from that container. He tipped it over. Objective reached — a fire at either end of the floor.

"Fire!" he hollered again as he approached Rachel's room for the second time.

A woman screamed in the distance. Patients, escorted by medical staff, whizzed past in wheelchairs and on stretchers.

Nick continued to hum *Happy Days Are Here Again* ... A chuckle escaped his throat as he watched the unfolding chaos. The floor emptied quickly.

He slipped into Rachel's room.

The over-head lights were off, but a soft night-light shone upon the bed where she lay, snuggled up in a large blue blanket. He walked over.

"Hey, *Rache*, it's me, wake up. I want to tell you how my life is going. *Rache. Rache.*"

He yanked the blanket off.

At that instant, a boot slammed into his chest. Nick flew backwards, crashing against the metal frame of another bed and dropped to the floor.

A young man jump out of Rachel's bed, holding a switchblade in his hand.

Nick scrambled to his feet. His fingers seized the gun he'd borrowed from the detective and pulled it out of his pocket.

The young man froze a few feet away.

Laughing, Nick pointed the pistol at the man's head. "Don't bring a knife to a gun fight, young fella."

The young man backed away and threw his knife on the ground.

Nick's eyes narrowed. "Okay, where is she?"

"I don't know."

"You've got five seconds to tell me. One ..."

The young man said nothing.

"Two ..."

"She's at home."

"You'll have to do better. Three ..."

"Nick, don't," Rachel said. She'd been hiding and watching from the shadows of the far corner of the room.

He turned. "Rachel, you *are* here. How wonderful."

Mark made a move, but Nick swung around, pointing the gun again. "Rache, come over and stand beside your friend.

"I can't really ..."

"Oh, they've got you in a wheelchair, huh?" He grinned. "Let me help you." Keeping the gun trained on the young man, he wheeled Rachel over beside Mark and then stood back a few feet. "Ah, that's better."

Sirens wailed outside. The blue and red lights of arriving emergency vehicles flashed through the window. Nick ripped off his cap and threw it to the ground, again pointing the pistol at Mark.

Rachel stared at Nick, transfixed by the bizarreness of everything. His face was pale and he had a small shiner. His eyes were frantic, and maybe even dilated. Together with his bald head, he looked insane. The lights flashing across his face gave an eerie feeling to the unfolding drama.

This was not the Nick she knew.

"And whom do we have here?" Nick asked.

"Mark," Rachel answered.

"Logan's son, I presume."

No one answered. Smoke drifted into the room.

Mark coughed. "Don't you think we should leave?"

Nick laughed. "Nice try. I've got nowhere to go this evening. How about you?"

"Did you see Logan?" Rachel asked.

"Yes, I'm afraid he's quite indisposed at the moment."

Rachel's pulse quickened. She felt hysterical. "What do you mean?"

"He's taking a nap — a long nap."

"Where?! What have you done?!" she screeched.

Nick threw he head back and laughed. "Revenge is so sweet."

"Revenge for what?"

"For what you did to me ... *and* my mother ... Big Apple ... turning Melanie against me. I know you've been texting her."

"Nick, I didn't do any of that. I never texted Mel after I quit. What has happened to you?"

He pointed the gun at her. "Why did you reject me — reject Mother's kind offer?"

"I ... I ...."

"For a lowlife indie author? You have really sunk, Rache. You had such great potential." He grinned. "I'm certainly better looking, smarter, and more successful .... Why did you do it, Rache? Why did you betray me? Why did you ruin my life?"

"I'm sorry, Nick. I didn't mean to, I just fell in love with Logan."

"Ah, *love*. Are you sure it's love, Rache? You loved me

at one point, remember? Maybe you're just infatuated with him ... but don't ask me why."

"I do love him, Nick. I —"

"Stop! I don't want to hear it." Nick raised his hands to his ears, the gun precariously close to his own head.

At that moment, Jonathan stole into the room with a gun in hand, a uniformed officer on his heels.

Nick noticed her eyes flinch.

Grinning, Nick lowered his hands, pointing the gun at Rachel. "The ole *someone is behind me* trick, huh? Do you think I'm that stupid —"

"Don't move. I'm Detective Chiu, and I have a gun pointed at you."

Nick's eyes popped, obviously startled by the change in events. He suddenly appeared nervous; sweat broke out on his forehead. He raised the gun to Rachel's head. "If you shoot me, I'll shoot her. It will be your fault."

"It doesn't work like that," responded Jonathan. "You will be dead before you hear or see anything."

"Oh, really? Would you like to bet on that? He squeezed the handle — his sweaty finger twitching on the trigger —

Blam! Crash! A bullet ripped through Nick and shattered the window on the way out.

Rachel screamed and covered her head with her hands.

Nick fell to the ground, landing right in front of her, his gun falling harmlessly to the side.

No-one moved for a moment.

At that instant, Nick grabbed Rachel's ankle. She screamed again.

"Did you ever love me, Rachel?" His voice was raspy.

Rachel bent down and pried his fingers away.

Blood pooled around Nick. "No-one ever loved me, Rache, not even Mother." His breathing became heavier. "I was an orphan, you know." He began to make gurgling noises.

Rachel stared at his face, transfixed by everything. "What?"

His lips twitched. He was trying to smile. "Good-bye, Rachel," he whispered, and was gone.

She began to sob. Not for Nick, but for everything.

Mark jumped over to her, hugging her tight.

Jonathan bent down and scooped his pistol, handing the other one to the constable. He holstered his gun and rubbed his head. "I've got a killer headache."

"Were you hit?" asked Mark.

"Yeah, he smashed me with a flashlight." Jonathan walked over and sat on the bed opposite Rachel's.

"You need a doctor," said Rachel, looking at him. "Did you see Logan?"

"No. Wait. I think there was a shot ..."

"*Oh my God*!" yelled Rachel.

Mark stared at Jonathan. "Da went looking for you."

"Quick, check the basement," replied Jonathan, lying down on the bed.

Mark stormed out of the room as a fireman and another constable appeared at the door. "We've got the fire under control," said the fireman, opening the shattered window.

"Good work," answered Jonathan, sitting back up. He

glanced at the constables and pointed at Nick. "Get this piece of trash out of here."

Mark raced from one end of the basement to the other, frantically looking for his father. As he searched room by room, he spotted blood on the floor outside a door. He tried to open it, but couldn't. There was something ... He pushed again. It was a body.

"Da, Da," he shouted.

At that moment, a couple of burly firemen marched down the hallway towards him. "Help me!" Mark hollered. "My dad is injured."

They ran and helped him push open the door. The older firemen dropped to his knees and grabbed Da's wrist. "He's alive. Looks like he's got a bullet wound to the abdomen. Let's get him to emergency."

Relief flooded through Mark. *He's alive! Thank you, Lord.*

The younger fireman found a blanket and laid it on the hallway floor. They loaded Da on it and carried him to the elevator. Mark raced ahead and opened the elevator for them. Soon they were at Emergency and placed Da on a stretcher.

Thankfully, the fire and smoke had not reached this area of the hospital.

A male doctor rushed out and examined Da. He spoke to a nurse: "Prep him for surgery stat."

Mark stared at the doctor. "I'm his son."

The doctor gazed at him. "There's no damage to any

vital organs as far as I can tell. He's lost a lot of blood though." The doctor sped away.

Mark marched to the elevator to break the news to Rachel.

19
The Spirit

Rachel, leaning on her crutches, stared at Logan and thought about how unfair life was. Was it not bad enough that the elderly man in the red Mustang had been killed (Bree had informed her), she, herself, badly injured ... Jonathan's concussion ... Lena terrorized? Did Nick have to shoot Logan as well? It was surreal to think that she'd been in a coma, and now, here she was, hoping and praying for her love. The surgery had gone well, but, of course, his injury had gotten infected. *Of course.* Logan now had a high fever. The doctor had given him antibiotics, but ... She shook her head and rolled her eyes. She was angry. She lifted her eyes, because she knew Who she was angry at.

Where was God?

Where was their protection?

Why would a loving God allow so much harm and suffering? She knew these were age-old questions, but this was *her* life. *Their* life. She was not feeling particularly Christian at the moment. She decided to go to the waiting area. She leaned over, kissed Logan on the cheek and walked out of the room and down the hallway.

Thankfully, the waiting area was empty. She paced, or rather, limped with crutches, as tears flooded her eyes. Words spilled out of her mouth. Thankfully, she was able to keep them to a whisper. "Where are you, God? What are you doing? How much can we take?" She raised a fist and shook it at God. "I am so mad at you."

More words came out of her. Angry, spiteful words. She shook her fist multiple times. She didn't care. God was going to hear from her. After a while, she felt exhausted and finally sat down on an orange plastic chair, crying. "I'm so mad at you," she whispered again. Her stomach actually hurt from the suffering she felt.

"Woman, why are you crying?"

Rachel's body flinched. The words startled her. She looked up.

A Black man gazed at her.

She felt so embarrassed. She reached for another Kleenex and wiped her eyes. "I'm sorry," she offered.

He sat down beside her. "Please don't apologize. I'm Pastor Tim. I've met you before."

She was confused. "You have?"

"Yes, I met your husband, Logan, and we prayed for you when you were in a coma."

"Oh my goodness. That's right. He did mention that to me. I totally forgot."

"It's okay."

Her eyes welled up again. She couldn't stop herself.

"Logan is ..."

"I know. He was shot."

She nodded.

"And we're going to pray for him, just like we prayed for you, because God is faithful and true."

"Sorry, I'm actually mad at God right now."

"That's okay. He can handle it. I get mad at Him sometimes too."

"You do?"

"Of course. God wants truth. He wants to share our joys, fears, pain, disappointment."

Rachel could see her mother in her mind – her greying hair and lively blue eyes. She could hear her saying those exact things. "Yeah, I guess."

"God wants real. He doesn't like fake prayers and fake religion. Something tells me you know that."

She nodded. "You would love my mother. She's in Heaven."

"That's a good place to be."

She nodded. There was silence between them for a couple of minutes, but it was not awkward. It was somehow right.

He laid a hand on her shoulder. "Would you mind if I pray for you and Logan?"

She rested her hand on his. "Please do."

20
The Crime Explained

All eyes were on Detective Chiu. Everyone sat in Bree's living room, waiting with hardly-concealed impatience for the sleuth to relate his findings.

Jonathan, sitting in the love seat beside Bree, sipped his coffee while balancing a plate with a half-eaten blueberry muffin on his knees. He looked good, recovering nicely from the concussion he had sustained in the encounter with Nick two weeks ago.

Rachel winced. It was still painful to think about that day.

She turned her head and glanced at Logan, who was sitting beside her on the couch.

He bit a huge chunk off his muffin and chewed heartily.

She smiled. His appetite was coming back. She was relieved to see him recovering so speedily after the emergency surgery. The wound was healing well.

She bent forward and picked up her cup from the coffee table, a movement that gave her no trepidation any longer.

The headaches were diminishing with every passing day.

She looked down at her leg. The cast, though, would be with her for a couple of months.

Rachel took a sip of coffee and put the cup back on the table, peeking over at Lena, who sat to her right.

Her friend was gazing at Jonathan.

Rachel couldn't suppress a smile. That girl was clearly smitten with him.

Jonathan finished his muffin and returned his plate to the coffee table.

"Another muffin, Jonathan?" Bree asked.

"Thank you, Bree, but sadly I have to say no." He smiled. "Two are my max. They were extremely tasty, though."

And so they were. It was nice of Bree to serve them freshly baked blueberry muffins, still slightly warm from the oven. For Rachel, it was a sign of much needed normalcy, a taste of home.

Mark leaned forward in his chair. "I think we're all bursting with curiosity, Jonathan. Please tell us what you know."

Jonathan nodded, took another sip of his coffee, and cleared his throat.

"I've been able to piece together Nick's history with the help of Detective Nichols. The mystery as to how he could have been here and back in the States at the same time has been solved. It turns out that Nick was adopted as a child."

Rachel let out a gasp and turned to Lena, who was shaking her head in disbelief.

"His biological parents were killed in a plane crash when

he was five years old. He and his older brother, William, who went by Billy, ended up in an orphanage and then eventually a foster home, but it didn't work out. They were sent back to the orphanage. When Nick was nine years old, and Billy was ten, the Hoffmans visited the orphanage looking for a child to adopt. They didn't want two boys, so the brothers were split up."

Jonathan pulled two print outs from his inside jacket pocket and laid them on the table.

"Here are the photos of Billy and Nick that were sent to me. They were taken a year before the adoption. You can see how similar they are. They look like twins."

Lena leaned over and picked up the photos. "Oh my goodness," she said. She showed them to Rachel, who just stared at them, shaking her head. Logan reached over and took her hand.

She squeezed his. The less she saw of Nick, at any age, the better.

Lena put the photos back on the table.

Jonathan took another sip of his coffee. "Nichols told me that Nick located Bill earlier this year and they planned this whole scheme in detail. Bill has been a career criminal — stealing cars, dealing drugs — so Nick paid him handsomely to help out.

"As a side note, the Miami police have been doing some digging into this case. It appears that Bill has assumed Nick's identity and has been draining his bank accounts. But that's another story.

"Back to this case. Nick and Bill boarded the cruise

ship together. Bill's last name is Davidson. Once on the ship, they simply exchanged passports, and Bill returned to America as Nick Hoffman, and Bill Davidson left the ship in Sydney to fly back to America to visit his ailing mother — except he never left Cape Breton."

"How did he get the car?" Logan asked.

"We think that Bill, the real Bill, paid some local low-life for a stolen car before he left. The vehicle identification number was filed off, so we couldn't trace it."

Rachel shook her head. "All this carnage for what? To get back at me?"

Jonathan nodded. "Yes. The family business going bankrupt, his mother's stroke, his fiancee Melanie leaving him ... In addition, we found some prescription drugs on him, probably supplied by Bill. Nick was in a bad state of mind. It all put him over the edge."

"I think he was unstable to begin with," said Lena, sliding her arm around Rachel's shoulders.

"I agree with that," answered Mark, and everyone nodded.

"What happens now?" asked Logan.

"We located Bill. He was hiding out in Miami and staying at Nick's condo. He's facing multiple charges and a lengthy prison sentence."

"Good," said Rachel. "Time to put this sordid mess behind us. I don't want to hear of them ever again."

Jonathan slipped the photos back into his jacket. "About those blueberry muffins?" he said with a smile. "I might make an exception today."

"Oh, yeah," answered Bree.

Mark rose to his feet, grabbed the bowl with muffins and passed it to Jonathan.

"While I'm standing, would anyone like a refill?" asked Mark, picking up his large mug.

"Sure, I'll take another cup" replied Logan.

"Yes, please," answered Lena.

Rachel saw Bree giving Mark an appreciative smile as he collected cups and headed to the kitchen. He was a good host and a marvellous husband, making sure his pregnant wife got the rest she needed. Rachel had no doubt that he'd be a terrific father too. A true protector, just like Logan — she'd never forget how they had acted in the hospital, selflessly being there for her in that perilous situation.

"I'd love to have another cup, but I've got to get going now,"Jonathan said, wolfing down the muffin.

"Are you sure you can't stay?" pleaded Bree.

"Sorry," he answered, glancing at this watch. "Busy, busy. I've got another case and have to give testimony in court. Seems like crime never takes a day off."

Logan reached over and shook his hand. "Maybe you can drop by for a meal and a game of cards one of these nights?"

Jonathan rose to leave. "That sounds great. I can't remember the last time I did something like that." He faced Lena, his face flushing. "Um, would you have a minute? I need to ask you ... something."

Rachel turned towards her friend. She didn't want to miss a minute of this development.

Lena blushed. "Sure. Here?"

"Um, well, maybe outside for a minute, if that works."

Rachel tried hard to suppress the grin spreading across her face.

Lena jumped up. "Of course."

Jonathan shook everyone's hand as they thanked him profusely, then he and Lena headed out the door together.

"Quick, quick, look out the window," whispered Rachel to Logan.

Logan turned, slowly. "Um, Honey, I don't know if we should ..."

Bree struggled to her feet and peeked around the curtains.

"What's going on?" asked Rachel.

"They're just talking," replied Bree, "beside Jonathan's car. Wait ... he put a hand on her arm .... Eek! They're kissing!"

"Eek!" exclaimed Rachel. "I knew it! Oh my goodness! Yay!" There, she had been right to tell Lena not to give up hope. And how wonderful that it had happened here on the island.

"She's coming back," Bree blurted, before slumping down beside Rachel.

The front door opened.

"There she comes," said Bree.

All eyes fell upon Lena as she re-entered the living room.

She stopped and looked around. "*What*?"

"What did Jonathan want?" asked Rachel coyly.

Lena pointed at her. "Wait, were you guys looking out the window?"

Everyone laughed.

"Yes, of course!" said Rachel.

Lena blushed. "He wants to take me out to dinner tonight."

Rachel stretched out her arms, beckoning with her hands. "Come here, my Dear."

Logan moved to the love seat, and Lena sat down beside Rachel.

They hugged.

"We're so happy for you," said Bree, wiping away a tear.

Lena sniffled and fumbled a tissue out of her pocket.

Rachel felt herself welling up too. What a glorious day it was.

"More coffee, Da?" said the smiling Mark heading to the kitchen.

"Yup," answered Logan, getting up.

21
New Beginnings

A dazzling August sun beat down upon Grace Baptist Church in Sydney River. The doors and windows of the small white church stood open to allow a refreshing breeze to flow through. The pews were filled with family and friends.

Dressed in a tan suit, Pastor Tim addressed the congregation: "Dearly Beloved, we are gathered here today in the presence of God, family, and friends for a joyous occasion, to join these two people in holy matrimony."

Rachel gazed deep into Logan's eyes, as he reached over and held her hand. Her love for him had only grown in all this time. They smiled at each other and turned back towards the minister.

"This sacred ceremony is a celebration of love, commitment, and the joining of two hearts and lives."

Lena looked radiant in her white long-sleeve dress and Jonathan as handsome as ever in a navy-blue suit with a vest. They made a beautiful couple, gazing at each other, overflowing with their love.

Rachel could not be happier for her, for them. If anyone deserved love, and had waited for it forever, it was Lena. It was as if a burden had been lifted from her soul. Rachel could see it in her eyes.

"Jonathan Chiu, do you take this woman to be your lawfully wedded wife, to love her, to honour her, to comfort her, in sickness and in health, forsaking all others, for as long as you both shall live?"

"I do," answered Jonathan.

Pastor Tim turned to Lena. "And do you, Lena Richards, take this man to be your lawfully wedded husband, to love him, to honour him, to comfort him, in sickness and in health, forsaking all others, for as long as you both shall live?"

"I do," Lena answered.

Jonathan placed the ring on Lena's finger. "I give this ring as a token of my love."

Lena did the same.

Pastor Tim beamed at the couple. "I now pronounce you man and wife."

The newlyweds stepped towards each other and kissed.

Sighs were heard throughout the church. As the ecstatic couple turned towards them, the congregation broke out in applause.

The simple ceremony now complete, the couple walked down the centre of the church to 'You Can Depend On Me' by Restless Heart. They smiled and waved to all the well-wishers, who stood.

Logan helped Rachel to stand, and she blew a kiss to the couple. Lena, catching her eye, blew her one in return.

When the newly-weds had exited the church, Rachel and Logan sat back down.

She sighed and gazed at Logan again. "I can't wait for our big day." They'd decided on a date in October when her leg should be healed, and she'd be able to walk towards the altar with the gracefulness due to the occasion.

Logan squeezed her hand. "Me neither. It'll be here before you know it."

At that moment, she realized that Logan was holding a small white box.

She smiled. "What's this?"

She opened it quickly, her eyes welling up. It was the exact replacement ring for the one that had been destroyed in the accident. Smiling, she lifted it out of the box and handed it to her love. "Oh, Logan," she whispered.

He slid it onto her finger, leaned over and kissed her.

"I love you," she said.

"I love you too — always and forever."

She grinned. "Hurry, let's get outside or we'll miss them before they leave."

Logan helped her to her feet and handed her the crutches.

They motored out of the church as fast as they could. Standing outside, beside Mark and Bree, they shouted and waved to the couple driving away with a *Just Married* sign on the back of Jonathan's blue BMW.

"Wasn't that lovely?" asked Rachel.

Bree sighed. "It sure was." She frowned, looking back

towards the church where the pastor was closing up the doors. "Mark, I need to use the washroom."

"Do you want me to walk you back in?"

"No, I should be fine. I'll just waddle up the access ramp."

Rachel chuckled. She watched Bree make her way back into the church through the door the pastor held open for her.

"Man, it's hot," said Logan as they chatted about the weather and the ceremony.

Mark glanced back towards the church entrance as he checked the time on his phone. "It's been almost ten minutes. I think I better check on Bree." He walked off.

A short while later, he marched back, frantically waving at Rachel and Logan. "Bree's water broke! What am I supposed to do?"

"Oh my goodness," said Rachel as joy flooded her heart.

"Pull up your car!" ordered Logan, patting him on the back and laughing. "You're on your way to the hospital."

"Oh my God!" shouted Mark, who didn't know whether to run back into the church or get the car.

"We'll get Bree," said Logan, *"go get the car."*

"Right," answered Mark, finally taking off.

Logan and Rachel chuckled and rushed back into the church, heading towards the washroom.

"Just think," said Rachel, "Penny might be born on Lena's wedding day."

"That's wonderful," replied Logan.

"Are you okay?" asked Rachel while Logan pushed open

the washroom door.

"Yeah, my water broke."

Rachel chuckled. "We know. I'm coming in."

Two hours later, Logan and Rachel were relaxing on the back deck when Logan's phone rang.

"Hey, Mark. You're on speaker so Rachel can hear too."

"Hi Rachel."

"Hey Mark."

There was excitement in Mark's voice, and some concern. "Bree's in labour for sure. The contractions are getting stronger. She's struggling a bit. The doctor told us it might take a while."

"Sounds pretty normal," Logan encouraged.

"Yeah, she's in some pain. I'm rubbing her back with a tennis ball."

"Good man," replied Logan.

Rachel leaned over. "She's going to need all your love and support."

"Yup, I'm here for her and Penny."

"Do you need anything?" asked Logan.

"No, I had clothes and sneakers packed in the car, thank God, so I changed."

"Good," replied Logan.

"Well, I should go," said Mark. "Will update you again in an hour or so."

"We're praying for you guys," said Rachel.

"Thanks, we need it."

They all said goodbye.

Just over two hours later, Logan's phone rang again. He and Rachel were relaxing on the couch, enjoying tea, cookies and a movie.

Logan answered, putting the phone on speaker again. "Hey Mark."

"Hey Da and Rachel. Bree's really pushing now. The doctor said they're going to do a Cesarean section."

Logan glanced at Rachel, who squeezed his hand. "That's how you came into the world," replied Logan.

"Really?"

"Yup, it's pretty standard today. Don't worry."

"Oh, good, I thought it meant something is wrong."

"Not necessarily, Penny is probably just stubborn and doesn't want to come out the normal way."

Mark and Rachel laughed.

"Thanks, Da, I gotta go."

"You're doing great, Mark," said Rachel.

"Thanks, guys. Bye."

At quarter after ten, the phone rang again.

Logan and Rachel had just climbed into bed.

"Hey Mark," said Logan.

"Congratulations, Da and Rachel. You're grandparents! Penny was born about fifteen minutes ago. She's beautiful. I held her. Mom's doing great. I can't believe it! We're so happy!"

"Congratulations, Mark!" Rachel shouted.

"Congratulations, Son," said Logan. "We're so incredibly happy for you and Bree. You'll make great parents."

"Thanks," replied Mark. "They put a little hat on Penny. Her head is a little pointy where she was trying to come out. The nurse said it will go away over time."

"Perfectly normal," answered Logan.

Rachel cuddled up to Logan. They were both beaming.

"Okay, I've got to go," said Mark. "I have to call her family and friends too."

"Yup. We love you Mark," said Logan. "Give our love to Bree and Penny."

"Love you, Mark," said Rachel.

"Love you, guys. Bye."

Logan put the phone on the nightstand and turned back to his love. They lay together, facing each other, massive grins on their faces.

"You're going to be a wonderful grandfather," Rachel said.

"And you'll be such a great grandmother. What do you want Penny to call you?"

"Hmm. Probably just Rachel."

"Nope, that won't do. How about Nana or Grandma? My grandmother was called Nana."

"Nana, eh? Yeah, I like it. I can't wait to meet her."

"We'll go to the hospital in the morning."

Rachel snuggled up to him. "Okay, Grandpa."

Bree, sitting up in bed, smiled at Rachel and Logan who strolled into the room. "Where are your crutches, lady?"

"I graduated," replied Rachel. "Enough about me, where is she?"

Mark turned towards them, cradling the baby.

Logan's and Rachel's eyes were glued to Penny.

"Oh, she's beautiful," remarked Rachel as Mark handed the newborn to Logan.

Logan beamed at his new grandchild. "My goodness, look at that dark hair."

"The doctor said it might change over time," said Bree.

Smiling, Rachel gazed at Bree. "She's got your blue eyes."

Bree grinned from ear to ear.

"She looks so much like her mom," said Mark.

After a couple of minutes, Logan gazed at Rachel. "Well, Nana, are you going to hold Penny?"

"Oh yeah." Rachel had such an incredible feeling when the baby was placed in her arms. She couldn't remember the last time she held a baby. "Oh, she's so beautiful," she repeated. "And she smell's so sweet."

"How much did she weigh at birth?" Logan asked.

"Seven pounds, three ounces," beamed Mark.

Penny started to cry. "Aww, do you need some milk?" asked Rachel, walking over to Bree.

"Yes, bring *Penelope Rachel Stewart* over here," replied Bree.

Rachel stopped in her tracks. "*Rachel*?"

"Yes," answered Mark, "we named her after this wonderful woman that we know and love."

Rachel gazed at Bree as she handed over Penny. "Oh, my goodness, I don't know what to say. I'm so honoured."

Bree smiled at her. "You don't have to say anything. We

love you. You know that."

Rachel reached over and squeezed her hand as her eyes welled up.

Logan took Mark into a bear hug. They slapped each other's backs. "Thank you, guys, that means a lot to us," Logan said.

22

A Rising Star

The Union Square Barnes & Noble in Manhattan was packed and buzzing. About three hundred eager fans, sitting in chairs, were waiting to hear from bestselling author, Amy Jones. You could feel the excitement in the air. Sporting a black sweater, she looked stunning in her new choppy lob haircut, with blonde streaks. The vast store was a bit chilly on this late-September evening.

Gazing at Amy, Rachel thought back on the past couple of days in the Big Apple — her old stomping grounds. Rachel, Logan, Lena, and Amy had booked fabulous hotel rooms in the heart of Manhattan and had made a mini vacation out of the trip. They took Amy shopping to the best stores on Fifth Avenue.

Rachel chuckled. Amy had been like a ten-year-old on Christmas morning. Lena and Rachel totally spoiled her. Logan was tagging along for the ride, but ducked into a few men's shops and bought a few items for himself.

The foursome ate wonderful meals at great restaurants

261

and even took in a play on the first night. Amy clung to Rachel's side like a daughter, and when Amy mentioned that she wanted to get a new hairdo for the big event, she timidly informed Rachel that she wanted a shag like hers. Rachel was honoured and told her that she knew the perfect place and that she was paying for it. In fact, Cove Island paid for everything on the trip for all four of them.

She came back to the present as she saw the female assistant manager walk up to the front where Amy was already seated. There were two chairs in front of the crowd with a small table on each side of the chairs. A large table stood about ten feet away with dozens of copies of Amy's book ready for signing.

The dark-haired assistant manager rushed over, picked up her microphone, and took her seat beside Amy. The young author was already wired up with a small mic attached to her sweater. The assistant manager shook Amy's hand and then faced the attendees.

"Hello, everyone, I am Michelle Gaines, the assistant manager of this wonderful store in this historic building. Thank you all for coming out this evening. We are so very pleased to have up-and-coming literary star, Amy Jones, with us. She's going to read from her new cozy mystery novel, *A Writers' Group Murder*, and then afterwards take a few questions from the audience."

The attendees clapped.

Michelle gestured to the large table. "After the event, Amy will sign copies at the table and then you can proceed to the checkout. Amy's new novel is rocketing up the bestseller lists. I've read it myself and can tell you that it is a wonderful book to snuggle up with on a rainy evening, or any time actually. So, without further ado, I present to you Amy Jones and *A Writers' Group Murder*."

The young author locked eyes with Rachel who stood in the back of the room — Logan and Lena on either side of her. Rachel smiled, raised her hand high and gave her an enthusiastic thumbs up.

Amy raised her eyebrows for a second and took a sip of her hot chocolate. Placing it back down on the small table beside her, she picked up her copy of the novel.

"Thank you, Michelle, for the introduction and for hosting this event tonight. It's my first public reading, so I hope I won't sound too nervous."

"You'll do great," replied Michelle.

Amy flipped through the novel to the page she'd bookmarked:

"Madeline's chair faced the large windows that looked northeast onto the busy street. Another flash lit up the sky in the distance, followed by more rumbling. The storm was moving away. She sighed. In Madeline's mind, it was the perfect day — a storm and sharing her story.

"Hi Madeline," greeted Agnes. "Good to see you."

"And you as well."

"Come and get it," Agnes said to the group, gesturing to her trolley.

Rain pounded on the roof. The lights flickered for a moment, and the room suddenly went dark.

"Oh, no!" exclaimed Mrs. Kovalchuk.

"I hate thunderstorms," remarked Lois.

"Me too," agreed Cindy.

"Don't worry, Lois," replied her husband.

"Calm down, everyone," Dr. Tollman said. "Stay seated. Everything will be fine."

"I'm going to check the breakers," a male voice bellowed from the hallway. It was old Joe Roach, the creepy caretaker of the building. Madeline didn't like him at all, and was somewhat afraid of the tall bald man, who often wore a ratty ball cap. A couple of months before, she'd tarried behind after a meeting, and he'd accidentally locked her in. After she complained, he stared her down before finally unlocking the door. She'd noticed the smell of alcohol on his breath as she squeezed past.

Waiting on Joe, the group patiently chatted away in the dark. Five minutes later, the lights came back on.

"Thank God," said Madeline and Lois at the same time. They chuckled.

"Thank you, Joe," Agnes hollered and turned back to the group. "Let's get our drinks and start reading."

Each member rose, grabbed a drink and cookies, and returned to their seats.

Taking her chair beside Madeline again, Agnes addressed the group. "Thank you all for coming again this week. I hope you had an inspired week and typed out many pages. Who would like to begin?"

"I would!" exclaimed Lois, beaming and shuffling her papers.

Agnes nodded.

Lois began: "My new novel is entitled Cabot Trail Mystery.*" She cleared her throat. "It was a dark and stormy night."*

Madeline chuckled inside herself as that opening line was the cliche of cliches. But she'd still listen intently to offer constructive criticism.

At that moment, Dr. Tollman grunted, gurgled and grabbed at his chest. As everyone turned their attention to him, his face smashed onto the table with a loud thud.

For a second, everyone stared in shock — then Agnes and Cindy screamed.

Mr. Quigley rose and rushed to the professor's side. He grabbed Dr. Tollman's wrist, and, after a minute, let it fall to the table. He stood stoically, staring straight ahead.

All eyes locked on Mr. Quigley's grave face as his lips moved: "I'm afraid Professor Tollman is dead."

Madeline's vivid imagination kicked into overdrive. She tried to stop herself, but it was hard. No, it was impossible. Her grandmother had warned her many times that Madeline's imagination would get her into trouble one day. Perhaps, but how could a person live without imagination? How could she live or write or breathe without imagining all sorts of wonderful things? This case wasn't wonderful, of course, but it was intriguing. Madeline decided that she'd proceed with solving this crime. For it must be a crime, mustn't it?

The professor had, no doubt, been murdered by someone in the group. The question was, by whom? And how could she find out? She studied each face. She immediately ruled out Mr. Quigley and his wife. Why would they want to kill the professor? They had no connection to him.

Her eyes rested on each person that remained, one at a time. Cindy Seaver wore a blank stare on her face. Madeline didn't read too much into it, though, as Cindy was a bit of an airhead.

Mrs. Kovalchuk, however, looked distraught. An act? The unfriendly widow, for certain, would be high on Madeline's list of suspects.

She glanced at the facilitator. Agnes had tears in her eyes. However, she could be one of those suspects that flies under the radar. Madeline had read enough Agatha Christie to know that. Madeline filed her initial thoughts into her mental notebook. Once home, she would jot them down in her physical notebook.

Mr. Quigley phoned the police and gave them as many details as he could. They were on their way.

Musing on events, Madeline sipped her coffee and nibbled on a chocolate chip cookie. How should she proceed? She wondered how the medical examiner would rule on the cause of death. In the meantime, she thought she might visit each member of the group at their residence — gain their trust and ask them penetrating questions. Whom should she visit first?"

Rachel looked around the room. Wow. You could hear a pin drop. The audience was intently listening to every word Amy spoke. It was amazing. She'd come a long way in a short time, soaking up all the advice that Rachel and Bree could give her. Rachel fondly remembered how the young writer had shown up with her father at the new office on that memorable Christmas Day.

As Amy continued to read, Logan wrapped his arm around Rachel's shoulders.

Rachel glanced at Lena who stood close.

Lena smiled and, perceiving her emotion, reached over and squeezed her hand.

Rachel's heart was truly full. Amy was blossoming into the writing star they'd envisioned. Her books were taking off across America, and the Cove Island team had scheduled a ten city tour for *A Writers' Group Murder.*

The New York Times and USA Today reviewers had raved about her new novel.

Logan's sales were also doing quite well in the Northeast of the US and on Amazon, but he was content to stay in the background for now, especially after the June madness with Nick.

She sighed. Mark had scheduled a relaxing tour of Atlantic Canadian cities for Logan's novels in December. Logan was also taking a greater interest in the publishing side of things and had been learning a lot from Rachel and Lena. It didn't hurt that Cove Island was turning a tidy profit on both sides of the border.

Were things finally settling down? She hoped so, because she and Logan were planning their wedding for October. They didn't want to wait any longer. They didn't need or want a big ceremony. She asked Logan a few times if he'd like to get married at Dominion Beach. She wanted a stress free simple wedding.

He was of the same mind, so one day they invited Pastor Tim over for lunch and discussed the possibilities. He thought it was a great idea and agreed to do the service.

She and Logan were spending lots of time with their granddaughter these days. Penny brought new rays of sunshine into their lives — lives that were full and overflowing with blessings. Rachel thought a lot about God these days. The doctors had told her and Logan that they probably couldn't have children of their own, and so, Rachel had prayed and prayed, but they were still not able to conceive.

At first she was disappointed, but had then thought a lot about Amy and Penny. It had dawned on her one day that God was giving her children and grandchildren, but just in a different way. She loved mentoring Amy, and traveling with her to book signings. Amy's dad, Fred, had entrusted Rachel with Amy's care on the trips. Sometimes Rachel would glance at her understudy and imagine that she was, indeed, her own daughter. Their relationship grew wonderfully, and Amy would ask her about hair, clothes, and thoughts on her boyfriend.

Life was what you made of it. Rachel was learning to be thankful and grateful and to count her blessings. As the old saying goes: when life gives you lemons, make lemonade.

Rachel came back to the present as Amy finished her final sentence. There was silence for a moment and then the room erupted in rapturous applause.

"Wow, what a response!" exclaimed Lena, stepping over to Rachel and Logan for a group hug.

"I knew they'd love it," whispered Rachel. "Bree told me it was her best work. I haven't read the last chapter yet, though."

"I won't spoil it for you then," replied Lena. "But it's wonderful."

The assistant manager announced that Amy would now take a few questions and then sign books.

Grinning, Amy locked eyes with Rachel again. Rachel blew her a kiss, and gave her two big thumbs up. She felt so content, and leaned back against Logan. Everything she wanted in life was right here. She wanted to stay in this moment forever.

23
Cruising

The wind blew through Rachel's hair as she took another corner on the Cabot Trail. She loved the new cherry-red Mazda Miata convertible that Logan had purchased for her with his royalty earnings. The sports car handled great — hugging the roads.

Rachel giggled with joy. The top was down and the weather perfect. Road after road carved through tree-lined hills, overlooking rugged cliffs and sandy shores. Red and gold leaves waved at them. The view was stunning. She'd always wanted to drive the Cabot Trail since that first cruise to the island, now here she was ripping through it with her new husband. Her husband. It was all so hard to believe.

They'd stayed in the picturesque French town of Cheticamp for the last few days, and today were stopping in the beach resort of Ingonish on the way back home. The entire week on the Trail had been refreshing. Rachel felt like a new person, and she knew that Logan felt the same.

As the road straightened out, Rachel glanced at Logan, then at her bridal set. She sighed, thinking back to the wedding, only a few short days ago.

They'd gotten married at Dominion Beach with a small group of family and friends: Mark, Bree and baby Penny, Lena and Jonathan, Amy, her boyfriend, Noah, and her dad, as well as Emma, the pastor's wife.

Rachel glowed in a stunning knee-length white summer dress while her bridesmaid, Lena, wore light blue. Logan was dashing in a blue tux jacket, blue jeans and sandals. Mark, dressed the same as his dad, stood in as his best man.

The theme of the wedding was for everyone to be relaxed — no stress. So, Rachel and Logan had planned a very simple wedding. Pastor Tim agreed to do the service at the beach.

At first, Rachel was hesitant to have the wedding at Dominion Beach because of the bad dream about Nick, but the pastor (whom she'd confided in about the nightmare) convinced her to fight against her fears.

"Who is Nick?" Pastor Tim had asked her. "Nick doesn't own the beach. Claim the beach. It is *your* special place, not his."

She loved his courage and faith. He was truly inspiring. Tim told her that he was praying for her everyday. One day, she had a breakthrough and decided she wasn't going to let Nick affect her life anymore. She told Logan she wanted their wedding to be held at Dominion Beach, and he was in full agreement.

It was a wonderful ceremony on a cloudy October day with a light ocean breeze. Thankfully, the sun broke through for the main part of the service. Rachel quietly thanked God for that. She also thanked Him for their health. She hadn't had a headache in weeks and her leg felt almost perfect. Logan also had no after-effects from his bullet wound.

Shortly after the wedding, they headed to their waiting car as their friends hooped, hollered, clapped and threw confetti all over them. Just before climbing into the car, Rachel tossed her bouquet over her shoulder. Amy caught it. Everyone congratulated her and ribbed Noah and her dad.

As they waved to everyone and drove off, Rachel was under the impression (from Logan) that they were going to a hotel in Bras d'Or for their honeymoon, but he surprised her. He'd made other plans, and had everything packed and ready to go.

"All the arrangements have been made," he said with a grin. "You just have to sit back and enjoy the ride. Each day of our honeymoon will be a surprise."

Before she knew it, they were driving the Cabot Trail. She'd told him many times that she'd wanted to do the famous circuit, and now, here it was.

She smiled, coming back to the present. Logan lifted his Tim's tea out of the holder and held it up for a cheers. She picked up her Starbucks cafe latte and tapped his cup.

"Here's to Cheticamp," he said. "I love that town."

"Me too. In fact, I've loved every town and beach that

we've visited on this trip."

He took a sip of his tea. "Wait till you see the huge waves in Ingonish." He glanced at her. "You're kind of short, they might go right over your head."

"Hey, stop picking on us short people," she joked, drinking the last of her coffee. "I can't wait to experience it."

They stopped at a few spots along the way and arrived at Ingonish Chalets just before supper. They checked in and soon opened the door to their rustic cabin, which was right across the road from the beach. The inside of the cabin reminded them both of Logan's old place in Low Point. It was wooden and cozy and they loved it.

After relaxing for a bit, they walked to The Caper Shack for supper. Rachel wore blue jean shorts, a white summer shirt and sandals. Logan sported a wine-red T-shirt, blue jean shorts and sandals. She gazed at him as they walked and held hands. He was looking sexier than usual after not having shaved for a couple of days.

"What?" he asked, noticing her staring.

"Oh, nothing," she answered, leaning into him.

They'd had their fill of fish on their honeymoon, so they both went for a steak and potatoes, and washed the meal down with a bit too much wine and beer. Afterwards, they decided to go for a small hike as night descended upon the quiet town — a quarter-moon hanging among the twinkling stars.

Walking hand in hand from the end of the trail to the main beach, they found it deserted.

"What a romantic evening," Rachel remarked, looking up at the moon and stars.

"Yeah, and still so warm."

She gazed at her love. "What time is it?"

He looked at his watch. "Just after ten-thirty."

"Wow. I didn't realize it was so late."

He smiled. "Yeah, we went to supper about seven-thirty."

"Right. We had a late lunch." She removed her sandals and ran along the sandy shore and into the ocean, just up to her waist. Surprisingly, the water was still warm. Logan charged in right behind her, hugging her from behind. She melted into his arms.

At that moment, a large wave passed through them, almost covering her.

"Whoa!" she exclaimed.

"Yeah, I told you. Ingonish is famous for these big waves. They'll keep coming."

She peered out, making out the rising waves coming towards her as the moon shone upon them. Another wave washed over them. It was an incredible experience.

Logan grinned. "Do you want to swim?"

She raised her eyebrows. "Just a little, we've been drinking." She giggled and dove in.

He laughed and joined her, both frolicking around, but not venturing out any farther.

A few minutes later, they strolled out of the water and sat down along the water's edge.

Rachel sighed. "This is so beautiful, Logan."

"Yeah, and so are you."

He gazed at her with those eyes beneath those bangs. He leaned over and kissed her, softly rubbing her shoulder. Soon, he was lying on top of her, kissing her lips, her shoulder, her neck.

A sigh escaped her throat. His hair brushed her face, his breathing became heavy. Hers too. He unbuttoned her shorts. She thought about stopping and trying to make it back to their cabin, but ... She felt the cool sand under her. Everything felt great. She gazed at him. All she could see was an outline of his head and hair with a backdrop of stars. It was hopeless. She was too far gone. Waves of pleasure crashed over her again and again.

They stayed in each other's arms for a few minutes afterwards, before he rolled onto his back — both of them breathless and staring at the stars.

She quickly shimmied back into her shorts.

"Wow," he said.

She giggled. "Yeah. A big item off my bucket list."

"Are you kidding me?" he asked.

They laughed.

She rolled on top of him. "Nope. But I had not really expected this one to come true." She kissed him softly on the lips, then laid her head on his chest.

24

The Final Chapter

A Writers' Group Murder
Amy Jones
Chapter 23

adeline drove her grass-green Chevy Spark the short distance from Sydney to South Bar along the New Waterford highway. The sea and sky were grey, and a few drops of rain pelted the windshield on the cool October afternoon. Madeline sighed. The red and yellow leaves filled her heart with joy. It was her favourite time of year.

Cindy lived on a hill overlooking the countryside and ocean. Turning right, Madeline puttered up to the side of the old wooden two-storey house. Faded blue paint was peeling in spots, and the yard was untidy. A rusted-out bicycle lay on the ground on the far side of the lawn.

She parked the car, exited, and walked up the small wooden steps to the front door. The left railing badly needed repair.

Madeline rang the doorbell.

A minute later, Cindy, wearing a thick grey sweater and blue jeans, threw open the door and smiled at her guest. "Welcome, Madeline, so glad to see you. Come on in."

"And you as well." Madeline stepped inside the small entrance area and removed her boots.

Cindy hung up her coat and waved for Madeline to follow. "Come on into the kitchen. Lunch is just about ready. I just have to take the soup off the stove."

The kitchen was bright with a large window revealing a deck and a lush backyard. Beige wallpaper printed with small violets adorned the walls of the room, giving off a 70s vibe. A wooden table stood against the wall, covered with a white tablecloth, a small pot of golden mums in the centre. Three padded chairs sat around it.

Cindy gestured towards the table. "Have a seat. Do you want to eat right away or have a cup of tea and a chat first?"

"I'd love a cup of tea," replied Madeline as she took her seat.

"I love your necklace," said Cindy.

Madeline cradled the pearl-drop pendant in her fingers. "Thank you. My grandmother gave it to me for my birthday."

"It's beautiful. And your black sweater shows it off nicely."

"Thank you."

Cindy poured and sat down. "Would you like a tea biscuit?"

"I'd love one." Madeline poured cream into her tea,

then picked up a biscuit and buttered it.

Cindy did the same.

"How about some fresh strawberry jam?" Cindy asked.

"Oh, yeah." Madeline applied a little.

Cindy brushed back a lock of hair. "I was so happy that you suggested we get together."

"Yeah, we've known each other for over a year now. I thought it would be good to get to know each other better."

"I couldn't agree more."

"I actually met with the other members recently also."

"You did?"

"Yeah. Ever since Dr. Tollman's death, I felt it my duty to keep everyone close and to check in on the members."

"That's so sweet of you."

Madeline sipped her tea. "Thanks. Plus I've been a bit curious ... about the death ..."

"I thought the medical examiner ruled it a heart attack — a natural death."

"Yes, that is correct."

Cindy rose. "Ready for lunch?"

"Yes, ma'am."

"Soup or straight to the clubhouse?"

"Is it a chicken clubhouse?"

"Yes."

"Oh, that sounds lovely."

Cindy brought Madeline a clubhouse and poured herself a bowl of soup. Madeline said a quick Grace inside herself. (Nana would never allow her to eat without giving Thanks.)

Cindy sat down. "So, you said you visited the other

members?"

"Yes, to tell you the truth, I was playing amateur sleuth until the police solved the mystery."

Cindy smiled. "Your very own cozy mystery."

Madeline giggled. "Exactly. I thought it would be fun and maybe I could get some new ideas for a novel." Madeline caught herself and stared at her host. "Um, I hope that doesn't sound too morbid or disrespectful to the professor."

Cindy smiled. "Not to me. Plus, I don't think it matters now."

"Hmm. My grandmother thinks I have an overactive imagination. I guess she might be right."

"Maybe."

Madeline gazed into Cindy's eyes. What was behind the maybe? *Was it nothing or was it something? In the bright kitchen light, Madeline could make out more wrinkles on Cindy's face than she'd noticed before. She always thought that Cindy was just shy of thirty, but now, perhaps mid-thirties. Madeline sighed inside herself. Despite the wrinkles, Cindy was incredibly beautiful, her sharp blue eyes a striking contrast to her thick red hair. It was hard not to be jealous. However, Cindy's eyes also seemed tired. She looked as if she'd recently cried.*

"Will the group continue on now?" Cindy asked.

"Yes, I suppose, although we did miss last week. I hope it will start up again soon."

"Would you like anything else?"

"More tea, please. This clubhouse tastes great."

"*Thank you.*" *Cindy served her and brought herself two sections of the sandwich. She sat again. "So what did your sleuthing turn up?"*

"*Oh, not much,*" *Madeline replied. "The Quigley's were as boring as the grandfather clock that ticked loudly in their living room.*"

Cindy chuckled.

Madeline smiled. That was, of course, a lie. But she'd promised Lois not to tell a soul of what she'd discovered about Mr. Quigley.

"*And Agnes was still in mourning, She was really shaken by Dr. Tollman's death, so I didn't get much out of her. However, Mrs. Kovalchuck was quite the surprise. She was very pleasant. She lives in a nice condo, just off Prince Street. I had her pegged completely the opposite. I think I have a lot to learn about human character.*"

Cindy raised her eyebrows. "Yeah, I would've thought she was a dark soul. She seems so negative, almost depressive."

"*Yeah, so I thought before I visited.*" *Madeline gazed at Cindy's innocent face. She hated to deceive her like this, but she didn't want to reveal what she'd discovered about Mrs. Kovalchuk.*

Cindy shifted in her seat. "So ... no crime and no suspects."

Was Cindy asking or stating a fact? It was hard to tell. Once again, Madeline thought she detected something in Cindy's eyes and in her voice. "Yeah, I didn't learn much at all. I made some notes after visiting the suspects, but, like you said, there was no crime in the end. And that spared me meeting with Joe Roach, who'd been last on my list."

Cindy nodded. "He always gives me weird vibes."

"Yeah, me too."

Cindy stared at her. "And what do you deduce about me?"

Madeline studied her face. "Um, well there is no crime now ..."

Cindy got up, poured more tea and sat down again. "Are you sure?"

"What do you mean?" Madeline asked, perplexed.

"Well, you have read Agatha Christie and Sherlock Holmes and other great detective novels?"

"Yes, of course."

"Well, sometimes the police get it wrong, and it's up to our hero or heroine to solve the mystery."

Still puzzled, Madeline asked: "Is there still a mystery here?"

"I don't know, perhaps."

"Hmm." Madeline had the feeling that Cindy was deciding whether to tell her something or not.

Cindy took a sip of her tea and smiled. "So, back to me. What do you deduce about me, whether there was a crime or not? I'm just curious."

"Well, you're very pretty ... and a lot smarter than you appear." Madeline instantly regretted her choice of words. "Sorry!"

Cindy chuckled. "It's okay. I know I come across as an airhead. Or at least, that's what others think of me.

Sometimes I play along, although I must tell you that secretly it offends me."

Madeline felt her cheeks get warm. "I'm sorry, Cindy, I didn't mean to offend you. It's just that you're so beautiful. Often, that doesn't go together with brains."

Cindy smiled. "No, I don't mean you. You have a good heart and are so refreshing, and so honest. But you know, I am well-read. I love to study and research. I spend a lot of time at the library. I'm not just a coffee barista. And I have written a novel."

Madeline's eyebrows raised. "You have?"

"Yes, I completed it two years ago, but after a bunch of rejection letters, just locked it away in my drawer of important papers. However, about a year ago, I took it out, dusted it off and read it again. It wasn't half bad. I adjusted it to become a cozy mystery and that's why I initially joined the group."

"Wow."

"Yes."

"Is that the one you're reading in the group?"

"No, I've kept this older one secret, because even though some agents turned it down, two agencies encouraged me — telling me it was a very good story. It just needed better character development."

Madeline smiled. "That sounds amazing. I'd love to hear it sometime."

Cindy brightened. "Maybe I could read you a portion while we have our tea."

"That would be lovely."

Cindy rose and disappeared into the living room. A few minutes later, she returned with a few pages in hand. She sat down and began to read.

Madeline was captured from the opening sentence and listened attentively. After a few pages, Cindy stopped. "What do you think?"

"I want to buy it!" blurted Madeline. "It's riveting and as good as any bestseller I get out of the library or buy at a bookstore."

Cindy laughed.

"I'm serious. You are such a good writer. No wonder you didn't want anyone to hear it yet. Someone could steal it."

"Someone did." Cindy stared intently at her.

"What do you mean? What happened, Cindy?"

"More tea?"

"Yes. Now tell me."

Cindy poured. "Like I said, I wanted to talk to you. I need to get something off my chest, but I have no real friends. No one I can trust." Cindy sat the pot down.

Madeline reached over and grasped her hand. "I'll be your friend."

"That's what I was hoping for," Cindy said as she squeezed Madeline hand in return. "I actually think you're the brightest, warmest person in the group. And, well, Agnes is nice and everything, but she's getting older and forgets some things."

Madeline held her gaze and tried to let Cindy know that she could trust her, whatever the issue was.

"Let's sit in the living room," Cindy said.

They carried their cups into the living room, which was dominated by a large bay window overlooking the countryside that rolled all the way down to the churning sea.

"What a great view," Madeline remarked. *She felt like the ocean today, her thoughts and feelings tossing and turning.*

"Yes, one of the very few good things about this old house." Cindy switched on two floor lamps. *Their yellow light gave the room a peaceful feeling.*

The friends sat down together on a grey cloth couch that had seen better days.

Black wing-back chairs stood at each end of the wooden coffee table, and a few watercolours of seascapes hung on the walls. There was also an old framed photo of a young handsome couple, perhaps Cindy's parents.

Cindy took a sip of tea and put down her cup on the coffee table. "Madeline, I have to tell you something. One day, about six months ago, after our writers' group meeting, Professor Tollman offered me a ride home."

Madeline nodded.

"It was so nice and warm, sitting in that expensive car — a classic blue Mercedes-Benz. I was tired of taking the bus all the time. It was so nice and warm. When we drove through the downtown core, heads turned, as people admired the car. I felt like a princess. Anyway, he drove me home that first time. We sat in the driveway and just talked for an hour. Well, that became a weekly ritual. I wish I

could go back and stop it, but ..."

"Then, one night, I invited him in for a piece of cherry pie and a cup of coffee. Part of me knew it was wrong, but I couldn't stop myself. I was lonely. I liked the attention. He was married, but whenever he spoke of his wife, it was in the past tense. He hinted that she was leaving him, that it was mutual. But in hindsight, I don't know if any of that was true."

Cindy rose and walked over to the window. She stared at the sea, tea in hand. "Then one night, he showed up at my door with a small bouquet of flowers, and behind his back, a bottle of wine. Against my better judgement, I let him in. We shared a glass of wine, and the next thing I knew, the radio was playing and we were dancing. I was so lonely." She sniffled. "I mean, the man was twenty years older than I, but having his attention, at that time, was something I couldn't resist. He was so knowledgeable and handsome. He dressed casually when he visited. The stuffy old professor from the writers' group was gone. His first name is Christian. I only found out that night. He said all the right things. We talked of our love of writing. After the second glass of wine, I pulled out my story and read the first chapter to him. He loved it. He told me how great it was. I remember that. We sat on the couch together."

Cindy returned to the couch and faced Madeline. "We made love that night. I could just kick myself. I'm so mad at myself. He made it sound so right. He was leaving his wife. He was falling in love with me. I thought I was falling in love with him also. I slept with him. I still can't believe I did it." Her eyes welled up.

Madeline reached her hand forward and patted Cindy's knee. "Oh, Cindy."

"Yeah, well guess what happened next? He left an hour later. He never called me that week, and the next time I saw him was at the writers' group. He offered me a ride home, as usual, but was unusually quiet. At my house, he came in for a piece of pie, but left a short time later. I felt empty. I felt angry. What was wrong? Had I done something wrong? I racked my brain. It took me a long time to realize that he just used me. I felt dirty. Used."

Tears rolled down Cindy's cheeks. She started to sob.

Madeline leaned over.

They hugged.

"What a creep," whispered Madeline.

"Yeah, and when I missed my period, I was horrified. I thought I was pregnant. Thank God, I wasn't. I was such a fool. A total fool."

"Don't blame yourself. He was a manipulator. I'm glad he's dead."

Cindy sat straight again. "No, Madeline. We mustn't say that."

Madeline was glad, though.

Cindy blew her nose, then continued. "Then, two months ago, he announced that he'd found that agent, remember?"

"Yes, I remember it well."

"Well, that was my story. He stole it. The description, blurb, word count, everything. He just changed the title and character names. It's my story. I felt so violated ... in

every way possible."

Madeline's eyebrows furrowed. "How despicable."

"Yes. To think he had snuck the manuscript out of my drawer and then come back that last time to put it back. Can you believe the gall of that man? I became very angry with him, and tried to think of what I might do. I didn't think anyone would believe me if I accused him to the group. Then, one day — that day — the opportunity arose. He dropped by the coffee shop, just like he used to do. I don't think he knew I was working. I was in the back getting supplies. He ordered a cafe latte, and I slipped two espresso's into it.

"I knew he had a weak heart, an irregular heartbeat. He'd told me that once. Well, I was so mad at him, that I spiked his coffee. And then I watched him have another coffee at the group, just before he died."

She stared at Madeline. "I killed him, Madeline. I killed Professor Tollman."

Madeline was shocked, at first, but then her detective mind kicked in. "Are you, sure, Cindy? I mean, are you sure those espressos would kill him?"

"Well, I tried to kill him, and he died right afterwards. The detective said that he had a lot of caffeine in his system."

Madeline rubbed her chin. "I don't know ..."

"You will have to turn me in, Madeline. I have confessed to murdering Dr. Tollman."

Madeline almost laughed. The whole thing seemed absurd. "Cindy, even if you did murder the professor, I don't think I could turn you in. He deserved it. It was kind of like self-defence in a way. I mean, he groomed you. Violated you. However you want to think of it. Plus, he stole your story, your life's work. What an evil man. Maybe you were temporarily insane."

Cindy sniffled. "Yeah, I don't think he was ever planning to leave his wife. I was just a conquest for him ..."

Madeline glanced at her watch. "I really hate to leave you, Cindy, but I have to get back to Nana. I'm supposed to take her shopping. I'll stay longer if you want me to."

"No, please take your Nana shopping. I'll be okay. Thank you for being a friend and for listening to me."

Madeline pulled out her phone. "Are you sure. I could just call her."

"No, you go ahead."

They rose together and Cindy retrieved her coat while Madeline put on her boots.

"I guess I'll know soon enough if you report me," Cindy said.

"Cindy, I'm not going to report you. I don't even have it straight in my own head. You've got my phone number. Call me if you want to talk or if you need anything at all."

"Thanks, Madeline."

They hugged, staying in the embrace for some time, and then Madeline left, waving out of the car window as she drove away.

On Saturday afternoon, an exhausted Cindy took the bus home after work and trudged up the long driveway.

As she looked up the road, she couldn't believe her eyes. Scaffolding was erected around her house, and people moved around her yard in a beehive of activity.

Closing in, she could make out the bees. Madeline was cutting the grass in the front yard with a reel mower while Agnes raked grass and leaves. Mr. Quigley and a young man sat on scaffolding at the far side of the house, scraping away old paint, and Lois stood on the front steps with her hands on her hips.

Madeline noticed Cindy approaching, stopped her work and faced her.

Cindy strolled up to her and smiled, with arms and hands outstretched. "What in the world is this?"

They embraced.

Madeline smiled. "Oh, just a few friends I gathered together to help spruce up your place. I hope you don't mind."

"Oh, I don't mind, considering that I thought I might be in prison by now."

"Let's never talk of it again, Cindy. Mrs. Kovalchuck is also coming. She should be here soon."

"Thank you so much, Madeline. You really are a caring soul."

Lois sauntered over. "I hope you don't mind, Cindy, but we brought some sandwiches for the workers and I put them on your kitchen table. We found a spare key under a flower pot on the back deck."

Cindy smiled. "Perfectly fine."

Agnes walked over and greeted Cindy, then raised her

voice for the men: "I think it's time for a break everyone."

With that, Mr. Quigley and the younger man joined them in front of the house. Mr Quigley said hello to Cindy, and then Madeline gestured to the brown-haired young man who was tall, thin, and about thirty-five years old.

"Cindy, this is my cousin, Tyler. He just returned home after working out west for a couple of years."

Madeline faced her cousin. "Tyler, this is Cindy, my friend from the writers' group."

Tyler and Cindy shook hands.

"Nice to meet you," said Cindy.

"Same," said Tyler, who was a man of few words.

Madeline grinned as her heart fluttered — her wild imagination leaping forward to match-maker heaven.

Cindy turned to the other ladies. "Lois and Agnes, can you please help me get the tea and coffee going?"

"Sure thing," they said in unison. The ladies entered the house as Madeline spent time talking to Alan and Tyler about painting the house, which would begin the next day.

Before heading inside, Madeline took a moment and gazed down the hill at the peaceful blue ocean and matching sky. She smiled. Even though it wasn't stormy, it was a great day.

Rachel sighed, closed the novel and laid it on the nightstand. She sat up, stuffing a second pillow behind her back, reading glasses still on her nose. "Logan, are you awake?" she whispered.

He mumbled something.

"Did you finish Amy's new book?"

"Yeah."

"What did you think?"

"Loved it."

"Me too, but what about the ending? Did you think Madeline should have turned in Cindy?"

"No."

"Would you turn me in, if I committed a crime?"

"Yes."

"*What*? You would?"

Logan's eyes opened. "What? Sorry, Honey, what was the question? I was still half asleep."

"Oh, never mind. I guess I'm just being silly. It's just a story, but it bothers me that Cindy got away with killing Dr. Tollman, even though he totally deserved it."

Logan leaned up on one elbow. "Oh, he deserved it. And no, I wouldn't report you or Cindy Seaver."

She smiled at him. "I guess I should turn off the light and go to sleep."

"Yeah, turn off the light, but I don't think I can sleep now."

Her eyebrows raised. "What do you mean?"

"Well, you're sitting there, looking all sexy with your glasses and nightie — all studious and everything."

"Oh yeah? You have a thing for bookworms?"

He grinned. "Yeah, for one in particular."

She clicked off the light and he pulled her towards himself.

The moon shone through the window just enough to let them see each other.

"Oh, you still have your glasses on?" Logan whispered.

"Yeah, I do."

"Good, I too have a bucket list."

"You do?"

"Yes." He softly kissed her lips and neck.

"Oh, Logan," she whispered, *"bucket list away."*

Epilogue

The sky was blue, the air frigid on Christmas morning. Rachel loved the sound of skates digging in and cutting the ice as everyone skated and played hockey on Cameron's Pond in Sydney River, just down the road from Grace Baptist Church. A light dusting of snow covered the small chapel, ground, and trees, giving a joyful, peaceful feeling to the special day.

Rachel, wearing a heavy mauve turtleneck with matching toque and gloves, focused on her main job at the moment, which was teaching Lena to skate. Rachel was on one side of her friend, and Bree held Lena's other arm. Directly behind them, Amy, wearing a thick blue sweater, pink hat and gloves, pulled Penny's sled around to howls of glee from the four-month-old, who had so many layers of clothing on, you could barely see her.

As they skated around the outer edge of the pond, the women gazed at the rambunctious men.

Logan, sporting the Leafs toque and scarf Rachel had

gifted him, passed the puck to Jonathan who skated in on Mark — decked out in full goalie gear — a blue Leafs jersey over a thick sweater. Like father, like son.

Jonathan, sporting a white Bruins jersey and black toque, fired a high wrist shot that found the top corner of the net above Mark's outstretched glove.

"He shoots, he scores!" yelled Logan as Jonathan raised his arms and stick.

Everyone hooted, hollered, and cheered.

Rachel softly elbowed Lena, who was bundled up in a blue parka. "I can't believe you don't know how to skate, given that you're such a big hockey fan — going to all those Rangers' games."

"I think I skated once or twice as a kid, but yeah, I could kick myself."

Rachel could see their breath as they spoke.

"You're doing great," noted Bree. "A lot better than when you started."

"Ha ha," replied Lena, who had actually fallen on her butt when she first came onto the ice. "I actually could use a rest," Lena said, "so if you want to join the boys, you can drop me off at the bench."

"Okay," said her helpers in unison as they assisted her to the bench and grabbed their sticks out of the snow bank.

Pastor Tim and his beautiful wife, Emma, showed up, and sat down beside Lena, lacing up their skates.

"Good morning!" the pastor shouted.

Everyone greeted him and his wife.

Soon, the couple glided over the pond together, holding

hands, and visiting with the skaters.

The girls raced over to the guys and hit their sticks on the ice, asking for the puck.

Jonathan passed it to Rachel, who passed to Bree.

She skated in on Mark, made a move and shot the black disc into the empty net.

"She shoots, she scores!" hollered Rachel.

Bree fired the puck back to her, and Rachel skated in on Mark. She shot the puck, but Mark made an easy save with his blocker. Undeterred, she jammed the rebound between his legs. "Yay!" she screamed lifting her stick.

"Girls rule, boys drool!" shouted Bree.

Everyone laughed.

Amy handed over Penny duties to Emma and skated over to the hockey players.

"Can I try?" Amy asked Rachel.

Rachel gave Amy her stick. "Of course. Have you ever played ice hockey before?"

"No, not really."

"Well, there's a first time for everything." Rachel faced Logan. "Would you like to do the honours?"

"Absolutely." Logan quickly taught her the basics, and in a short period of time, Amy was happily shooting pucks at Mark.

Pastor Tim skated up to Rachel. "So, how was Christmas morning — I mean earlier?"

"It was wonderful. We went over to Bree's shortly after we got up and opened presents together."

"Nice. God is good."

"Yes, it was a very tough year that somehow turned out good."

He smiled. "God has a habit of doing that."

"Yes, I've noticed. Everyone is invited to our place for hot chocolate after the skate. Are you and Emma coming over?"

"Of course. We can't stay long, though."

She gazed deep into his eyes. "Tim, I just want to thank you and Emma for all your support — your prayers, wisdom, visits."

"It's our pleasure."

They hugged.

"Okay, everyone," Logan finally shouted after another half hour of skating, playing hockey and pulling Penny around, "who's coming over for hot chocolate?"

"Me, me," rang out all over the pond.

"Okay, let's go!"

Everyone sat down on the benches and changed into their cold boots.

Mark and Jonathan carried the heavy red net over to the church garage, and then everyone hopped into their cars and trucks and headed for the Stewarts'.

A half hour later, everyone was settled in Rachel's living room. Mark, Tim and Emma sat on the long couch in front of the bay window, Lena and Jonathan on the love seat, and Logan in his big leather recliner.

Penny lay on her blanket to Logan's left, and Amy, sitting on the floor, entertained the baby with her favourite plush animals.

A crackling fire warmed the cheerful, talkative guests and thawed their frosty fingers, ears, and toes.

Rachel was so happy to finally have a full house at their new home. After serving, she and Bree brought in a couple of extra chairs from the kitchen. Rachel sat beside Amy and Penny and surveyed the room.

The lit-up tree and decorations looked and felt wonderful. Family portraits donned the walls, including new ones of Penny. Rachel gazed at the painting of Cove Island that hung above the fireplace. She sighed, thinking of how much her life had changed in the past two years. She took a moment and reflected on each person.

Bree, sitting to her left, had become her best friend. At times, she seemed like a sister, and at others, like a daughter.

Mark, like his wife, was a friend and yet, a son — and a fierce warrior.

Tim: a humble and courageous man of God.

Emma: beautiful inside and out — a warm and generous spirit.

Lena: her other best friend. She glanced at Lena's ring. She was *so* happy for her. She'd never seen Lena so content.

Jonathan: another warrior, smart and handsome, the man God had brought to Lena at the perfect time, and the man who'd saved Rachel's own life.

Her eyes met Logan's. There were no words to describe what he meant to her. Maybe *Everything*. He was, no doubt, reading her mind, a smile on his face. Her heart was full. She smiled back. She was so in love. God was so good.

Amy had Penny giggling as she showed her each animal and toy. Rachel studied the young writer's sweet face for a moment. The daughter she never had.

Amy turned and gave Rachel a warm smile.

Rachel sighed and reached over to Penny. The baby grabbed her finger. Penny's hair was turning more blonde each day. She was becoming a mini Bree.

Penny giggled again and so did Rachel. Babies were a sign of new life. A new day. A new beginning.

Rachel sat back up and looked straight ahead. Her eyes met Pastor Tim's. He smiled and took Emma's hand. She also gazed at Rachel.

"Would you mind if we sang a Christmas carol?" she asked.

"That would be lovely," Rachel replied.

Joy to the World
Emma started.
The Lord is come
her husband joined in.
Let Earth receive her King
everyone sang together.
Let every Heart
Prepare Him room
And Heaven 'n nature sing
And Heaven 'n nature sing
And Heaven 'n nature sing.

"That was absolutely wonderful," Bree remarked, and

everyone agreed.

"You have an incredible voice," Lena said to the pastor's wife.

"Thank you," Emma replied. "God is good."

Encouraged, Emma led them in 'Hark! The Herald Angels Sing' and 'Silent Night'. Not everyone knew all the words, but it didn't matter. Emma and Tim made everyone feel included. Smiles were on every face.

Fifteen minutes later, Tim and Emma announced they had to leave. "We've got three people from church joining us for lunch and a couple of street people," said Tim.

"We also have to get going," announced Jonathan.

Everyone rose to hug one another and shake hands.

"Merry Christmas," rang out as the guests left and headed to their cars.

Ten minutes after that, a red pickup truck pulled into the driveway.

"Da's here!" exclaimed Amy, looking out the window.

As Fred walked up to the door, Logan threw it open. "Merry Christmas!" said everyone to Fred as he entered.

"Merry Christmas!" he returned.

After Amy put on her coat and boots, Rachel handed her a card.

"Thank you," said Amy.

"Open it," Rachel replied.

Amy did and pulled out a piece of paper. "What's this?"

"That's a statement of your royalty earnings for the last quarter. It has already been deposited into your bank account."

Logan beamed as Amy handed it to her father.

Bree and Logan strolled over.

Fred stared at the statement and scratched his head. "This must be a mistake."

"Nope," a grinning Rachel replied.

"*Fifty thousand dollars*?!" exclaimed Amy. She grabbed her father's arm. "We can buy a new truck or a new house."

"Well, certainly a good down payment," chimed in Mark.

"Merry Christmas!" exclaimed Fred again.

Everyone wished him the same and hugged Fred and Amy, who then talked her dad's ear off on the way to the truck.

Rachel and the gang waved as Amy and her dad turned the truck around and left.

"That was incredible," said Logan.

"Yeah, that's what Christmas is all about," answered Bree, and everyone agreed.

Mark, Bree and Penny stayed and joined their hosts for a light lunch.

Afterwards, Bree laid Penny down for a nap in the spare room and returned to the living room.

Rachel put the chairs away and poked her head back in. "So, who wants to play a game of Hearts?"

"I do!" exclaimed Bree.

Everyone headed for the kitchen and their seats.

Rachel checked on the turkey, and then threw a deck of cards on the table.

"A beer?" Logan asked Mark.

"Oh yeah!"

Logan grabbed two Canadians, handing one to Mark and sitting down.

Rachel turned to Bree, who sat against the wall. "Wine, my Dear?"

"Yes, ma'am!"

Rachel poured two glasses and sat down across from Bree. Logan was to her left.

"The turkey smells great," Mark said, and everyone agreed.

Rachel took a big swig of her wine and thought back to the first time they'd played Hearts at Bree's.

She turned to Logan and grabbed his arm. "Is this the game where you give away your heart?"

Logan leaned over and laid his hand on hers. "Yes, but it's too late. You already have."

Rachel leaned over and they kissed.

Mark winked at Bree, who was smiling at him, and began to deal the cards.

ACKNOWLEDGEMENTS

I would like to thank:

Silke
for editing, graphic artwork, and typesetting

Nora Campbell & Mitzi Hathway
for their encouragement and support

Early Readers:
Leslie Ann MacIsaac, Pearl Egdell,
Priscille Belliveau, Sandra MacDonald, Susan
Odo, Darlene Desveaux, Alice Quigley

Proofreaders:
Jill Corley & Maria Ayala

Thank you for reading!

Please leave a rating and/or comment at Amazon.ca or Amazon.com

For more information about
our books, please visit
randalljamesbooks.com

Other Books by Randall James

Memoirs

Cape Breton Orphan

Cape Breton Orphan Returns

Youth & Family

Jace Power & the Battle of Mars City

Jace Power & the Rebels of Jupiter

Gold & Sharpe

Tyler Hicks & the Battle of Alpha Centauri

The Strikerz

For more information about

Randall James

and his books, please visit:

randalljamesbooks.com